Surprised Daaay

Timberwood Cove: Book 2

Liam Kingsley
© 2019
Disclaimer

Contents

Chapter 1 - Linc

Timberwood Cove was my idea of heaven on earth… Except in December. The cold was so brittle it turned me into a stiff, cranky old man. The mornings were the worst, and this one was no exception. I stayed in bed for as long as I could, bundled up in wool blankets pulled up to my nose. I watched flecks of dust float off the timber beams above my bed every time there was a *thud* coming from upstairs in my son Cole's room. He and his best friend Liam had learned to wrestle quietly, lest they wake me, but an occasional, *"Hey, no fair!"* echoed through the floorboards.

I turned my head to look at the clock beside my bed and groaned when I saw it was well and truly breakfast time. I'd have to feed the boys before they got overly hungry and irritable, and attacked each other for real. I hauled the heavy blankets back, inhaled sharply as the cold hit my limbs, and pulled myself out of bed. I felt like I was getting a premature preview of old age even though I was only thirty. I bent over to touch my toes, just to prove to myself I was still flexible, and groaned as I felt my lower back aching. Maybe it wasn't such a premature preview after all.

My joints became a little more limber as I took a searing hot shower, dressed in jeans, a heavy flannel shirt and a warm wool sweater, then trotted downstairs to the kitchen.

"Breakfast!" I called behind me, and immediately heard Cole's bedroom door fly open followed by a stampede of nearly nine-year-old feet on two flights of stairs. They were fast. They pushed past me, got to the breakfast table, and sat up straight before I'd even made it through the kitchen door.

"Wow, who are these well-behaved boys?" I smiled as I turned on the stove to warm up a pot of overnight oats.

"Just two cool kids who deserve really cool Christmas gifts." My son, Cole, shrugged nonchalantly.

His best friend, Liam, nodded enthusiastically as I placed mix-ins on the table in front of them.

"Excited for the holidays, huh?" I gave Cole a kiss on the top of his head and he gave me a big cheesy grin as he reached for the milk and poured himself a glass.

"Yeah!" Liam said, then he proceeded to eat a spoonful of butter. He'd been eating weird stuff ever since his alpha dad, my best friend Jaxon, had bitten him to turn him into a shifter. Butter was a new one, though.

"You're going to have a new baby sister or brother, Liam. What more could you even *want* for Christmas?" Cole asked before he took a big gulp of his milk.

"Um, a new bike. Duh," Liam said like Cole was an idiot.

Cole rolled his eyes. "That is not as cool as a *sibling*," he insisted, looking up at me accusingly. He'd been expressing his jealousy about Liam's *new sibling* since Liam's omega dad had become pregnant nine months ago. I'd thought it would be a phase that passed, but it had just become more intense as the due date drew closer. Cole's nagging had hit a fever pitch because Liam was staying over at our house while his dad, Bryce, was in the hospital giving birth.

It wouldn't be so bad, except his nagging was just echoing what I felt too—I wasn't exactly *done* with having kids, but I had been deeply, pathetically single for a long time.

"Well..." I cleared my throat as I spooned out the oats into our bowls. "Good things come to those who wait."

"I'm *eight*," he sighed, putting his chin in his hand. "I've been *waiting*."

"Do you complain to your mom about this too?" I asked as I put the bowls in front of them.

He nodded, immediately taking a big spoonful of the oats before hissing from the heat and spitting them back out.

"And what does she say?" I asked, genuinely wondering how my ex, Nicole, dealt with him.

"She says that Paco is my little brother," he grumbled as he poured cold milk into his bowl, and I let out a laugh.

"Paco *is* a cool dog," Liam interjected, blowing on a spoonful of his oats and taking a tentative bite.

"Yeah but he's also *crazy*," Cole said.

"You're both right," I agreed. "That husky is full of personality, and he's also got some...uh...mild behavior issues."

"Mild!" Cole exclaimed. "He ate my astronomy magazine last week! Like, the whole magazine!"

"Well, who says a brother or sister wouldn't also be crazy?" I asked while spooning peanut butter and jelly on top of my oats.

"Imagine if a baby ate a magazine," Liam said.

"Imagine if a magazine ate a *baby*." Cole giggled and Liam broke out into a fit of laughter.

The conversation degraded into imagining objects eating other objects, and I enjoyed the oats warming up my insides until Cole came back around to complaining about not having a sibling.

"Alright, playtime. Go run out back to warm up while I chop some wood," I said as I stood and pointed to the backyard.

Spoons immediately hit the edges of their bowls, chairs were practically thrown backward, and the two boys were outside before I'd even blinked. I grabbed my coat from beside the back door and headed out after them.

The branches of the Douglas fir trees and the ponderosa pines in the backyard were whirring around in the wind, and I watched as the boys' long hair blew wildly around their heads. They laughed and sprinted across the yard toward the woods. As they hit the tree line, I watched as both boys shifted into their wolf forms, clumsily falling over their long legs and wildly blundering toward the forest that separated our homestead—the Timberwood Cove Country Club—from the human side of town.

I was surprised to see Liam shift as he hadn't been able to do it yesterday, as far as I knew. But I was glad to know he'd finally managed after months of trying with Jaxon helping him. It could sometimes be difficult for humans who had been bitten to learn how to shift for the first time, but it seemed Liam had got the hang of it now.

I pulled on my boots, and then trudged out after them, making my way to the wood shed just off the side of our porch while bracing against the freezing cold wind.

Chopping wood warmed me up, but it also made my arms ache like a bitch. I was relieved when I felt my phone buzz in the back pocket of my jeans—it was Jaxon.

"Everything all good at the hospital?" I asked as I balanced the phone between my ear and shoulder and gathered a day's worth of wood in my arms.

"Perfect," he said, sounding incredibly proud. "It's all done. Bryce did an amazing job. We've got ourselves a baby girl."

"Congratulations!"

"Thanks, Linc," Jaxon said, sounding proud. "Is Liam doing alright? Think he'll be okay with a new baby sister?" There was a hint of worry in his tone now.

"Are you joking? That kid is the most well-balanced creature on the planet. He's ecstatic about the new addition to your family. It's Cole we should be worried about, he's jealous as hell." I moved the wood to one arm and started toward the door.

"Your boy loves having Liam over to play, so yeah, I can understand him wanting a brother or sister of his own," Jaxon said. "Hey, I have to go in. Bryce is ready for visitors, so can you bring Liam by?"

"Of course. We'll see you soon."

I stopped at the back door and let out an ear-piercing whistle and watched the tree line. In an instant, the boys came tumbling through the scrub, fur matted and stuck with twigs, mud, and leaves. They shifted back into their lanky human forms as they ran up to the porch.

"Inside!" I said, holding the door open. "Showers! Clean clothes! Make it snappy—it's time to hit the hospital!"

Liam's face lit up and he looked at me excitedly. "Did Dad…"

"Yep, you've got a baby sister, kiddo," I said and he laughed happily before sprinting inside.

"And you," I said, grabbing Cole's sleeve as he tried to slink past. "You have a new friend. She's going to need you to look after her for the rest of her life. That's nothing to turn your nose up at."

"It's not the same as having a *sister*," he grumbled.

"How would you know?" I asked with a smirk.

He gave me a stink-eye and stomped into the house. I rolled my eyes and followed him in. After dropping the cut timber by the wood burner I added a few logs to the glowing embers so the house would be nice and warm when we got back. Then I helped the kids get ready.

***

The drive to the hospital wasn't long, but Cole managed to pack in so much awkward conversation it seemed like it took a thousand years to get there.

"If Jaxon and Bryce have just had a baby, wouldn't it be the *best* time for *you* to have another baby? Then they could grow up together and be best friends like Liam and me. Right Liam?"

I glanced in the rearview mirror and raised my eyebrows at him.

"Uh, yeah probably," Liam said with a shrug, clearly not wanting to be pulled into Cole's plot.

"See, Dad." Cole gestured to Liam like he was scientific evidence.

"Unfortunately, I can't just *have a baby*—procreation doesn't work like that."

"So? Get a mate."

"Uh, that's not as simple as it sounds either," I said, and felt my heart sink a little, deeply wishing it *was* that easy.

"Why don't you just get back with Mom then?" he asked as we pulled up to a red light.

"Oh shit, that reminds me—" I reached for my phone.

"Dad! Don't text and drive!" Cole stretched over the back seat and slapped my hand. I pushed his shoulder and smooshed him against his door as he laughed and squealed until the lights switched to green and I turned back to drive.

"You text her for me then," I said, tossing the phone into his lap.

"Okay, what do you want me to say?" he asked.

"Tell her that Bryce has given birth and ask her to spread the news."

"Here's what I've got," he said, clearing his throat. "Dear Nicole, our son is so awesome. Let's have another awesome baby—"

I growled and snatched blindly at the phone, and he broke out into a fit of hysterics. As we pulled into the hospital, I searched for a parking spot as Liam threw off his seatbelt and body slammed Cole.

"Hey!" Cole yelled and laughed as he kicked his legs. "Traitor!"

Liam laughed and elbowed him in the ribs until he was able to snatch the phone out of Cole's grip. They were an even match in size and weight, but Liam had a bit of a speed advantage. The fight was over by the time I pulled up and parked.

"Here, Linc," Liam said, handing the phone to me over my shoulder.

"Traitor!" Cole repeated, making a last-effort grab for it before I snatched it and shoved it in my jeans pocket.

"Alright, cubs. Where are we?" I asked in my "serious alpha" voice as I turned to face them.

"The hospital?" they asked in unison.

"Right. And there are rules when we're in the hospital. What are they?"

"Touch everything," Cole said with a snicker.

"Talk *super* loudly about *everything*!" Liam suggested.

"Shift into wolves and—" Cole laughed and couldn't continue because he was laughing too hard. I waited patiently.

"Shift into wolves and run through the halls at top speed!" Liam said to finish Cole's sentence, and then he joined Cole's hysterics. I took a deep breath and let out a quiet but serious growl. They immediately pulled it together and sat upright.

"Touch nothing," I growled. "Stay quiet. And *there are no wolves in Timberwood Cove.*"

"There are no wolves in Timberwood Cove," they both said at the same time, repeating the credo.

"Once more," I insisted, coaxing them with my hands.

"There are no wolves in Timberwood Cove!" they said louder.

"Duh, of course there are no wolves in Timberwood Cove! Are you *crazy*?" I grinned at both of them. "Alright, good job. Let's go and meet this new addition to the pack. I mean, *family.*"

Cole and Liam giggled and we clambered out of the car.

The minute we stepped into the hospital, I was hit with the smell of anesthetic and a whole lot of stuff I didn't want to identify. My stomach turned. It wasn't often that I cursed my heightened senses, but a hospital was one place I'd rather *not* be. I choked back a gag and glanced down at the boys. They seemed completely un-phased and I wondered if their senses hadn't fully developed, or if they just didn't yet know to associate the smell of iron with blood, guts, and gore. I held back another surge of nausea and was about to walk quickly down the halls to Bryce's room before I felt Liam tug at my sleeve.

"Linc… Can we go in there?" he asked me quietly as he pointed to the gift shop.

"Balloons!" Cole yelled. "We have to get balloons, Dad!" A nurse and a woman in a wheelchair craned their necks to see what the fuss was about and I gave them an apologetic smile.

"Uh." I hesitated, wanting to get the hell out of there as quickly as possible, but Liam's face was beaming up at me with pleading eyes and Cole was already racing across the linoleum floor to a huge stand of helium-filled balloons.

"Well, sure," I said, resigned. "But let's keep it snappy."

I stood deep in a flower-filled corner of the gift shop while the boys debated about which balloons were best, and I took the opportunity to call Nicole.

"Hey good lookin'," she answered. "You feeling clucky?"

I frowned, not sure what she meant. "Uh, me?"

"Your texts sounded like you were hot for momma," she said, amusement lacing her tone.

"Oh shit." I laughed and ran a hand over my face. "Uh, sorry about that. *Cole* is impatient for a baby brother or sister… We're at the hospital."

"Wow, you move fast! A new baby already? Who's the lucky omega?"

I laughed again. "It's Bryce!"

"Ah, wow. Send my congratulations to him and Jax. Everything went okay, right?"

"Yeah, it sounded like it when I spoke to Jax. We haven't met the baby yet—in fact we haven't made it further than the gift shop," I said as I watched Cole shaking his head at Liam's suggestion of a Batman themed balloon. "That's what I called about though. Could you spread the word about our newest pack member?"

"Yeah, honey, you *know* my finger is ready to speed dial my girls the moment you hang up."

"I'm counting on it," I said, smiling.

"Hey, *get down from there!*" she shouted. "Oh my god, Linc. This *dog* is out of control. Hey, tell Cole he can have a new sibling after he trains Paco to stay off the breakfast table."

"So, never?" I chuckled.

"Right. Oh man, now he's eating my cereal. *No, Paco!*"

"Dad! Look at this!" Cole called across the shop at me, holding up a balloon covered in stars and galaxies.

"Gotta go, we've made a balloon choice," I said to Nicole.

"Good, and I need to research doggy obedience schools," she grumbled.

"*Dad!*" Cole yelled. I hung up the phone, grabbed an oversized bouquet of roses from the flower corner and made my way over to where the kids were holding way too many balloons. It looked like they could float up to the ceiling at any minute.

"Cool," I said, nodding to Cole's selection of space-themed balloons. They weren't exactly appropriate to congratulate a new baby or her dads, but Cole was so obsessed with astronomy I knew there was no arguing with him. Liam held more appropriately themed balloons—one shaped like a teddy bear, another one with bright sparkles reading "CONGRATULATIONS!" and a few that were filled with confetti.

"Which ones are your favorites?" I asked.

"All of them," Cole said.

"All of them," Liam echoed.

"Alright," I said, resigned. I paid for all of them, as well as the huge bouquet in my arms. I kept my nose pressed close to the flowers as we hurried down the halls to Bryce's room, pleased by how well the roses blocked out the smell of the hospital. Just as we turned a corner I saw Greer, our previous pack alpha, carrying a couple of colorful bags.

"Greer, hey," I said as I walked up to him. "Come to see the baby?" Of course he had, and by the grin on his face he couldn't wait to see his first grandchild.

"Yeah. I got a call from Jaxon saying they're ready to take visitors."

"Well, come on then." We both continued down the hall, Cole and Liam skipping ahead, barely stopping themselves from running, but they knew my rules, even though Cole hadn't particularly obeyed the no yelling rule.

However, the second I walked through the hospital room door I didn't give a shit about the rule.

"We come bearing gifts!" I announced as we paraded into the room. "Now let me see that baby girl!"

Jaxon's face lit up as we came in, and a huge smile broke across my face as my gaze fell on the tiny bundle in his arms.

I felt my wolf whining in my chest, and a strong paternal energy moved through me. I heard Liam gasp, and for once, Cole was quiet.

"Hey guys," Bryce said from the bed, waving to us weakly. Liam rushed over to his omega dad for a hug, and I felt Cole pressing himself against my hip as he gazed at Lori.

As I wrapped my arm around Cole's shoulders, I heard a soft voice mutter, "I'll get out of your way in a moment," and I looked up to find a nurse standing by Bryce's bed.

My eyes locked on the angle of his cheekbones, his freckled skin, and the slightest hint of golden stubble on his jaw just behind his ear where he must have missed shaving that morning. Everything else disappeared. I felt lightheaded. My wolf wanted me to sniff harder at the air, but I resisted. No way was I going to take a deep inhale of that hospital smell. And besides, it was probably nothing but the surging hormones of everyone in the labor and delivery ward that was making me feel so damn attracted to this human omega...

But as the nurse moved past me on his way out of the room, I couldn't help but catch a whiff of something unique, something I'd never smelled before. My wolf's attention was sharp and I felt it surge forward in my chest. I turned to watch the nurse walk away.

Chapter 2 - Shawn

A pitiful whine escaped from my sweet corgi's snout as soon as the eggs sizzled in the frying pan. She knew a treat was coming since I gave her a little piece of my breakfast every morning when I finished eating. She didn't want to wait, though, and tapped her little paws on the kitchen tiles impatiently.

"Be patient, LuLu my love," I said to her.

She sat down but kept her eyes fixed on the stove, licking her chops as I stirred the eggs into a fluffy scramble. When ready, I slid the eggs out of the pan and onto the toast already sitting on a plate. I reserved a small piece of egg for LuLu, then drizzled hot sauce on the rest and sat down at my kitchen island. LuLu followed me and sat next to the bar stool I was perched on. She gave me her best puppy eyes, her little eyebrows pinched together, and her adorable face cocked to the side.

"You're too much!" I said to her in between bites of my breakfast. Once I had scarfed down my portion, I grabbed LuLu's eggy treat and squatted down in front of her.

"Paw?" I asked, prompting her.

She gave me her paw to shake.

"Good girl! Other paw?"

She gave me her other paw, then stood up and wagged her tail expectantly. As a Cardigan Welsh Corgi, she had a natural bushy tail that hadn't been docked at birth, and I loved the way it swished in the air over her back.

"Here you go, sweetie," I cooed, extending my palm with the egg in it. She rushed forward and gulped it up without any hesitation—or chewing.

"Yum! You liked that, didn't you?" I asked her. I kissed her forehead and she ran off through her doggy door to use the facilities in the backyard while I hit the shower.

Emerging from the steamy bathroom with a towel around my waist, I heard my favorite song playing softly from the clock radio on my bedside table and dashed over to turn up the volume. It was repetitive and simplistic, but the hook was irresistible, and I shook my booty all over my bedroom, even convincing LuLu to join in with me, taking her front paws in my hands and twirling her around. Song over, I headed back to the bathroom, and then lathered up my face with shaving cream and started to shave, double checking that my sideburns were perfectly straight, meticulously rinsing my razor after every stroke. I got deep satisfaction out of my grooming routine and didn't like to miss a step. Once my face was perfectly smooth I rinsed with cold water then applied an unscented aftershave before starting on my hair. With a few pumps of mousse distributed evenly through my blond curls, I was looking fresh and ready for the day. All that was left was to pull on my scrubs and sneakers, and then get LuLu ready for doggie daycare.

Dressed and ready to go right on time, I grabbed my coat from the closet and wrapped a scarf around my neck, then grabbed LuLu's pink plaid leash from the hook by the door. She came bounding to meet me, wiggling her butt around in excitement as I unlatched the deadbolt.

"Ready for walkies at the park?" I asked her.

She gave one joyful bark.

"Ready to see all your furry friends at doggie daycare?"

This time she was so excited she wiggled herself around in a three hundred and sixty degree spin and then jumped in the air.

Her happy dance was just too much for me. My heart bursting with love, I scooped her up and cradled her in my arms, smushing my lips into her furry forehead to give her a flurry of kisses. Once I had fully opened the door, LuLu practically threw herself off the stone steps leading from my door to the sidewalk, scrambling to get her stumpy legs underneath her again when she landed on the pavement.

The dog park was just across the street, but I always kept LuLu on her leash until we got there. I just couldn't let my precious baby cross the street on her own, even in a small town like Timberwood Cove. She pulled on her lead for the entire twenty second walk across the street, and even though technically she wasn't *supposed* to do that, I couldn't blame her for being excited. She loved meeting other dogs and romping around in the grass.

As soon as we entered the gate of the dog park, a black toy poodle ran up to LuLu and sniffed her thoroughly. LuLu returned the favor, and they started circling each other with their curious noses.

"Hello, Little Miss Poodle, what's your name?" I asked her. I looked around but couldn't tell if any of the humans in the park were looking after her. A few metal tags jingled on her green collar, so I reached down to pet her head and tried to read her name off one of the tags. One of them said "DEMETRIA" with a phone number listed below. Demetria pushed her soft, tiny head back into my palm for more pets. LuLu, getting jealous, pushed the little poodle out of the way and took the role of accepting my affection.

"LuLu, you princess. I was just getting to know your new friend. No need to be rude."

Both dogs started licking my hand, so I squatted down to give each dog one hand and keep everyone happy.

"Demi!" A high-pitched voice yelled from across the park.

I looked up to see a young girl of maybe eight or nine in pink leggings and a gray puffy jacket running toward me and the two dogs.

"Sorry she jumped up on you, we're still trying to teach her not to do that," the little girl said.

"That's okay. No harm done."

"No jump, Demi!" the girl said to her poodle, who was now jumping on *her*, leaving muddy paw prints on her jacket and licking her face.

A man wearing baggy blue jeans and a black hoodie strolled up behind her holding a leash.

"We better put Demi back on the leash, Lyla," the man said to the little girl. "She's gonna get herself into trouble soon with her aggressive licking."

He reached down to clip the leash onto Demi's collar, but LuLu ran behind my legs and Demi had decided the chase was on. They rushed around us in circles, yipping at each other.

"Sorry," the man said to me.

"It's fine, really," I replied. "I think they like each other."

"Yeah, seems like it," he agreed. "I'm Dave, by the way."

"Hi Dave, I'm Shawn." I extended my hand to shake his.

"What's your puppy's name?" the girl asked.

"That's my LuLu."

"She's *so* cute!" Lyla squealed. "She has such tiny legs!" She reached out to pet LuLu but LuLu was still busy being chased by Demi.

"Thank you. I love her little legs too. Your Demi is adorable. She looks like a puppy, how old is she?"

"She's eight months old," Lyla answered. "So she's still *kinda* a puppy. But she's gonna stay small when she grows up."

"How long have you had her?"

"Um…" Lyla looked up at Dave. "I don't remember. When did we get Demi, Dad?"

"It was right after Papa's birthday, remember? So about three months ago."

At the word "Papa" I felt a pang in my heart. I had completely given up on having a family of my own. Phillip, my ex, left me because I wasn't able to conceive a child. We'd tried for six months, and when I didn't become pregnant he blamed me. Insisted I must be infertile because it wasn't him. I'd accepted I couldn't have children, that some things were just not meant to be, but times, like now, it hurt. Actually, considering my job, I had moments when it hurt nearly every day. At least I had LuLu, my furry baby.

"Nice to meet you, Shawn, but we've gotta get going. Time for school, Lyla," Dave said.

"Nice to meet you guys, too," I said with a smile. "See you around."

Lyla waved at me as they headed off to the other side of the dog park.

***

A bell chimed as I pushed open the front door of Pampered Paws Doggie Daycare.

"Miss LuLu, you are looking gorgeous this morning," exclaimed the daycare's owner, Trevor. Trevor's broad frame was swathed in a bright pink gingham button-down shirt and a matching pink pashmina around his neck, which probably would have clashed on someone with bright red hair but seemed just right on him.

"Isn't she just," I said, smiling at my pretty little Corgi, with her brilliant white snout and caramel colored eye patches. Her big ears tilted forward when she heard Trevor's voice and her mouth fell open to a big, panting grin.

"Don't think I've forgotten you too, handsome. You're looking a treat yourself today, Shawn." Trevor pointed his index finger at me while waving it around in a circular motion. "How do you get your hair to look so good? I swear there's not a curl out of place," he exclaimed with his hands out, fingers spread in gesture toward my head.

Trevor walked around from behind the counter and took LuLu's leash out of my hand, wrapping one of his arms around me and kissing my cheek.

"I just use a good mousse," I said.

"Whatever you're doing, it's working for you." Trevor's grin was as wide as the Cheshire Cat's.

"Now, I need to tell you something." Trevor's grin dropped as he grabbed my forearm. "Someone has recently seen wolves near the wooded area of town, by the golf course."

He said it so calmly, I frowned. I would have thought he'd be in hysterics about learning of wolves in the area.

"Wolves?" I asked skeptically. "I've never seen a wolf around Timberwood Cove. And why the heck would they live near our town when there's plenty of perfectly good woodland and mountains all around? Who saw them?"

"I don't exactly know, I overheard two customers talking about it at the florist when I went over there yesterday to complain about a horrible banging noise. God! They were doing some kind of construction and it was driving all the dogs crazy barking and growling. So I stormed over there to ask them to quiet down, and *Jason*"—Trevor said the name with extra disdain—"told me they were *just finishing up*. Bullshit. Of course, it went on for another hour. That man is so rude to me," Trevor said with a sigh and a shake of his head.

I waited patiently for him to swing the conversation back around to the wolves.

"Anyway, I wouldn't let this little party sausage out of my sight if I were you," he said with eyebrows raised and an index finger subtly pointing to LuLu, who lay on the floor with her chin resting on Trevor's shoe. She didn't seem to be buying into Trevor's scare tactics either. "Except when she's with me, of course. You don't need to worry about that. Our fencing is wolf-proof."

"Uh, I don't think we need to sound the alarm just yet," I objected. "Most people don't have the experience with animals that you and I do... They might have just seen a Husky or a German Shepherd and thought it was a wolf."

"Mm, maybe," Trevor said "But this isn't the first time it's happened. Need I remind you that wolf *shifters* are rumored to live in this region?"

"Seriously, Trev?" I groaned and rolled my eyes at the mention of the great mythical cryptid of the area.

"Well, you never know. I mean it's just a rumor, but..." Trever lowered his voice to a whisper. "Can you *imagine*?"

"Yeah. I can imagine life getting pretty chaotic if that turned out to be true," I said in a monotone voice.

"Mm. Chaotic and...*sexy*."

I burst out giggling. "I think you've been reading too many romance novels."

"Maybe *you* haven't been reading enough of them."

"Doubtful. Remind me, *how* did we get from a wolf sighting to acting like shifters exist?"

Trevor suddenly dropped his gaze as if he realized he'd probably said too much about something he shouldn't have said anything about, but if there *were* wolves or large stray dogs sighted in the area, he'd been right to warn me.

"Anyway, all I'm saying is... You can't be *too* careful," Trevor insisted.

"Oh, you know how careful I am with this priceless angel. You don't have to worry." I said to my friend. "I've got to scoot off to work now though, don't want to be late."

"Of course, you go take care of the miracles of human life. Leave the canine with me."

Trevor gave me a warm hug before turning his attention to LuLu. "Alright, Miss LuLu, let's go join the rest of the party animals out back."

"Thanks for looking after her," I said to Trevor.

"It's always my pleasure, honey," Trevor replied, then he shooed me off to work with a wave of his hand.

***

The labor and delivery wards were buzzing when I arrived. There were only three free rooms, and I estimated they'd all be full by the evening. Babies seemed to arrive en masse during a full moon for some reason, an odd pattern I'd noticed over my years as a registered nurse. I stuffed my coat into my locker, washed up, greeted a few coworkers at the nurse's station, and set off on my rounds.

First on my list was a cheerful woman named Deborah who was blissfully breastfeeding her newborn when I walked in the room. Deborah had a thick head of red hair pulled up into a bun and her baby also had the wispy starts of red hair on his precious little scalp.

"Good morning, Deborah! My name is Shawn, I'll be your nurse today."

"Hello," Deborah answered with a sleepy smile. "You can call me Deb."

"Sure thing," I replied, making a note on her chart. "How is this gorgeous little firecracker doing this morning?" I indicted the baby with my pen.

"He's a dream," she said. "Just eating and sleeping and screaming. That's normal, right?"

"As long as pooping and peeing are on the list too, yes, that about covers it."

Deborah chuckled. "You're very chipper for someone who has to talk about poop at work."

"Ha, well, it's all part and parcel of the job. I just love to see a new family enjoying sweet moments like these. It's a major perk," I answered honestly. "Anything I can help you with?"

"Could you just scoot that glass of water a bit closer to me?" she asked.

"Of course," I said, rolling the overbed table to where it was within easy reach.

"Thank you so much," Deb said.

"Of course. Just call if you need anything else. I'll be back later to take your vitals, alright?"

She nodded and beamed at me.

"Okay, see you, Deb!"

Next on my list was a guy called Terrence. I walked into the room to see a handsome black man with a shaved head and a closely trimmed goatee scrolling through his phone while he relaxed in bed.

"Good morning, Terrence. My name is Shawn, I'll be your nurse today," I said, just like I did every day, with every patient.

"Hi, Shawn," Terrence replied quietly, pointing at the cot next to his bed, where a fat, round-faced baby lay on their back, fast-asleep.

"Oh, bless," I said, lowering my voice and putting a hand over my heart when I saw the angelic infant. "What's the little one's name?" I asked.

"We named her Farrah," Terrence said with a soft smile that melted my heart. "Isn't she beautiful?"

"She's *stunning*. And such a cute name. Congratulations."

Farah really was stunning. Her lips were shaped like a little heart, her eyebrows were two perfect little black arches over her closed eyes, and her brown skin was smooth and flawless.

"Thank you," Terrence replied.

I glanced over at the screen of his heart monitor and scanned his chart. "Okay, your heart rate is looking great, I'm just going to check your blood pressure now, okay?"

"Yep, let's do this." Terrence sat up higher in bed.

"I know these things are annoying," I said apologetically as I pushed up the sleeve of his gown and wrapped the cuff around his bicep. "But I'll be done before you know it."

"You're the friendliest face I've seen in this hospital yet, so you won't hear me complain," Terrence said with a smile.

"That's very sweet of you to say," I replied as I pumped air into the cuff. I noted down his blood pressure in his chart, loosened the valve on the gauge to let the air out of the cuff, and declared him healthy.

"Alright, all systems are go, so unless there's anything else you need, I'll see you later, Terrence."

"Nope, I'm good. Thanks, Shawn."

"Always a pleasure. Call if you need me."

The rest of my rounds continued as usual. I made my way down the hall to my last patient's room. Bryce Baldwin.

"Good morning. Sorry to bother you. My name is Shawn. I'll be your daytime nurse today. I just need to check your vitals."

"Sure thing," Bryce said. I got him to hand Lori over to the man I assumed was his alpha, who cradled her with the confidence of someone who had handled a lot of babies, and I got to work checking Bryce's vitals.

I was fitting Bryce with a blood pressure cuff when two men and two children laden with bags, balloons and flowers came strutting into the room, with one of the men yelling, "We come bearing gifts!"

I looked up, frowning at the man who had yelled. Suddenly the air seemed to thicken, and I felt unexpectedly dizzy as if I wasn't receiving enough oxygen. I dragged my attention back to the task at hand, focusing on reading the sphygmomanometer as I released the air out of the cuff, but as I recorded the results on his chart, the dizziness increased, and an intense energy seemed to fill the room. I felt like I was pulled right into the moment, and everything around me came into sharp focus. I was impossibly aware of the man who had called out when he arrived, still standing near the door as one of the children came running up to Bryce for a hug. I didn't dare turn to look at the man, but from my earlier glance I already knew he was tall and incredibly broad shouldered with thick arms and strong muscular legs. And his eyes… Wow, they were gorgeous.

Stunningly attractive man aside, I was actually worried my blood sugar level had dropped or something, and there was only one thing that would help. "I'll be out of your way in just a moment," I said, finishing off writing up Bryce's vitals.

I hurried out of the room and went about gathering up the paperwork I needed to dole out before I could take an early break and eat some much-needed lunch.

Chapter 3 - Linc

I blinked hard to get the vision of the omega nurse out of my mind. As soon as he left the room, the intoxicating scent was gone and the hospital stink came rushing back. I tried to clear my head with a deep inhale of the roses and glanced around the room, looking for a window to open. Jaxon was holding the baby down low in his arms so Cole and Liam could meet the new arrival.

I walked out of the room for a moment, just to see if the nurse was definitely the source of the delicious smell, but when I looked up and down the hallways, he'd gone. A little confused, I walked back into the room Bryce was in.

"Anyone else overwhelmed by the smell in here?" I asked, scrunching up my nose at Jaxon.

He raised his eyebrows and cocked his head to the side. "Are you saying my daughter *stinks*?"

Bryce chuckled and Cole let out a laugh that was more like a yelp. I groaned and rolled my eyes.

"The *hospital* smell. I can't be the only one grossed out by it," I mumbled, taking another deep sniff of the roses.

"The medication they gave me dulled most of my senses," Bryce said as he wrapped an arm around Liam who was sitting on the side of his bed.

"It is a *strong* smell," Jaxon said. "It's not unusual for shifters to have certain smells that throw them off more than others. Maybe hospitals are yours, Linc. I knew someone who couldn't handle the smell of Tony's Pizza."

"You're kidding me."

"Yeah, couldn't set foot it in the place. Never ate a pepperoni pizza in his life."

"No way!" Cole said, sounding heartbroken at the idea of it.

"Yes way," Jaxon said solemnly before turning to me and gesturing to the newborn baby in his arms. "Here, take this bundle of joy. She'll take your mind off it."

Jaxon reached out and placed Lori in my arms as I handed the bouquet of flowers to Cole to hold. The moment the newborn babe landed in my arms, my heart started racing. Her tiny body seemed simultaneously fragile and powerful. Slowly, her eyes opened and she looked up at me with bright, star-filled eyes.

"Wow." I gazed down lovingly at her puffy cheeks and tiny button nose.

Jaxon was right. She *did* take my mind off it. Any feelings of nausea and repulsion from the smell of the hospital had been replaced by a strong, undeniable surge of longing.

"She's pretty special, isn't she," Bryce said with a glowing smile.

"Is she ever." I smiled back, but my heart was aching. I was happy for my best friend and his mate, but I couldn't help but feel a searing, grumbling ache of jealousy deep in my guts.

As if picking up on my inner longing, Cole let out an impatient sigh. "I want a little sister!"

"I know," I replied stiffly.

Lori closed her eyes again and opened her mouth to take a deep yawn and I felt like my heart broke into a million pieces from how cute it was. It was undeniable that Cole wasn't the only one who wanted another addition to the family—I was clucky as hell and frustrated beyond belief that I still hadn't found true love, a mate. I'd loved Cole's mom, Nicole, but she wasn't my mate, and soon after we'd had Cole, we realized we worked better as friends and co-parents than a couple, and we'd split amicably. My own parents hadn't been particularly pleased about that, insisting I should have stayed with Nicole. I think it was because I'd disappointed them that I hadn't actively sought out anyone afterward, hence it being more than eight years since I'd been with anyone. During that time I'd dedicated my life to looking after Cole, to raising him as a good alpha father should.

Suddenly, I felt my wolf pawing at my chest. At first, I put it down to my thoughts on finding a mate, but then that same head-spinning, intoxicating scent flooded into the room just as the nurse came back into view. Our eyes locked. My wolf practically lunged forward and it took all of my might to stay standing. I clutched Lori closer to my chest where my heart pounded.

His eyes held mine. His lips parted. I took a deep breath and bathed in the scent as it moved through and around me. Hair stood on the back of my neck and goosebumps broke across the skin of my arms.

And then, as quickly as it happened, it ended.

"Alright, Bryce," he said as he turned to look at the exhausted man in the hospital bed. I blinked hard to clear my head as he continued talking. "Everything is looking good. The doctor has signed off on your discharge paperwork, so as long as there are no complications, you'll be able to get out of here with your newborn tomorrow morning."

"Thanks, Shawn," Bryce smiled sleepily.

"We just need you to sign off some consent forms, and then I'll take you through the care information for leaving tomorrow."

"Can't he leave sooner than that?" Jaxon asked as he took Lori from my arms.

The nurse looked up and, again, our eyes locked for a moment, but then he looked away to address Jaxon.

"No, I'm afraid not," he said. "It's procedure to keep new babies and their parent at least overnight for monitoring. Didn't your midwife talk to you about this?"

"Uh…" Jaxon glanced back and forth between the nurse and me. I looked at Greer and then at Bryce, and found that they and the kids were also looking between the nurse and me. Our wolves were hyperaware that something was going on, though to be honest, I don't think any of us knew exactly what it was.

"It's just to give your system time to clear out the anesthetic," the nurse explained, a touch of nervousness in his voice. He glanced between the six of us and must have assumed our silence was in resistance to Bryce having to stay overnight. He swallowed and glanced around.

"Well, alright," Bryce said, breaking the tension. "Is the food good here, or what?"

"Oh of course. It's great," the nurse said before giving Bryce a grin. "And the snack machines are well-stocked."

"Can't wait," Bryce replied. He signed the paperwork and handed Shawn back the pen. I felt my chest clenching. I watched as the nurse put the pen in his pocket, gave us all a polite smile, and left.

"What the fuck was that?" I whispered, glancing at Jaxon with wild eyes. "Did you feel…"

"Go," Jax said, putting his hand on my shoulder and urging me forward. I didn't have to be told twice by my pack alpha to follow my intuition.

My wolf sniffed at the air, and I followed the intoxicating scent; followed the nurse. He walked quickly down the halls, long-legged and with confidence. His white sneakers gripped the slippery linoleum, while my boots had me skidding around corners and almost falling over myself in an effort not to lose him this time.

I watched the way his dark blue scrubs clung to his ass. My mouth filled with saliva as I gazed at the way the fabric moved back and forth across his hips as he walked. I rushed to keep up with him, my breath rasped as my throat tightened with desire. I took a sharp inhale, desperate for another hint of his scent—just as he rounded a corner and disappeared into a doorway. I followed him without thinking, and immediately smacked against him, barely stopping myself from falling over.

"Oh, hey!" he said, grabbing my shoulders and keeping me upright as I stumbled sideways.

"Oh geez, I'm sorry." I quickly righted myself, just about melting into the feeling of his hands on my shoulders when he let go.

"No problem. It's fine, but are you alright?" he asked, looking over my face. He peered into my eyes and I felt another rush of awareness, stronger now I was so close to him, but his expression wasn't reflecting anything of what I was feeling. He looked concerned, as if I might be sick or something.

"Yeah, I'm alright." I ran a hand through my hair, trying to act cool, but in reality I was shaking inside, all my senses on full alert. This man was *special* to me.

"You were just in Bryce's room, weren't you?" he asked, stepping back and cocking his head to the side.

"Oh, yeah, I'm close friends of Jaxon and Bryce. I'm Linc."

"Nice to meet you, Linc. I'm Shawn."

He held out his hand and I immediately took it. I inhaled sharply as his fingers curled around my hand, and that's when I knew for definite what was going on. Who Shawn was to me. A shiver raced up my spine, and my wolf yipped in barely contained excitement.

It was unmistakable. It was what everyone had told me it would be like—a deep knowing, a clawing need, an intense desire to *claim*. This nurse was my *fated mate*.

"I'm just about to take my break so…" He let go and motioned to the room behind him, which I realized was the nurses' break room.

"Oh, yeah, of course." I smiled and motioned to the snack machine on the wall behind him. "I'm just here to grab some snacks for Bryce."

"Careful of anything on the second row," he said as he wandered over to a couch. "It's been known to jam the machine up pretty bad."

I plunged a hand in my jean's pocket, searching for change as I wandered over to the snack machine. "But that's where all the good stuff is," I said as I glanced through the glass at the paltry selection on offer.

"You like buffalo jerky and cold salami sandwiches?" he asked skeptically.

"Actually, I do," I said, hoping it might provoke further conversation. However, when I looked over at where Shawn was sitting and unpacking a lunch bag, he wasn't paying the slightest attention to me. He was clearly a human, which was just my luck. Human's didn't have the capacity to pick up on the same signs as shifters. They didn't sense their mate or detect that unique fragrance their mate gave off. To him, I probably just smelled like my Dior Homme cologne and wood smoke from the heater at home. He probably thought I was a complete lunatic chasing after him down the halls, but if he just *knew* what I did we wouldn't have to do these ridiculous human mating rituals that took *so* long.

I took a deep breath and turned back to the snack machine. The least I could do was actually get Bryce something to eat while I pretended nonchalance. Avoiding the second row, I chose an egg salad sandwich for Bryce, and a bag of potato chips each for Cole and Liam. I glanced over at Shawn as I fed quarters into the machine and watched as he completely ignored me.

I grabbed the food from the tray at the bottom of the machine and took my time standing up. What the hell was I supposed to do now? Leave and miss my chance at connecting with my fated mate? No way. Not a chance. Plus, I had alpha orders. Even if I did manage to drag myself away from Shawn without so much as his phone number—what would Jaxon have to say about it?

Jaxon… That gave me a great idea. I made my way over to Shawn and was a second away from inviting him to hang out with me and my baseball superstar best friend when I was rudely interrupted.

"Dad!" Cole rushed into the room with Liam hot on his heels. "I've been *looking* for you!"

"*Shh,*" I hissed. "There are sleeping babies in this ward!"

"Lori just slept through me kissing her face a *thousand* times," Liam said.

"Well, Lori's special," I remarked, before turning to Shawn. "Sorry."

"It's quite fine," he said, wiping his mouth with his napkin. "Most newborns can sleep through anything."

"*See?*" Cole insisted. I growled under my breath and was resisting the urge to disown him when he looked right at Shawn's lunchbox. His eyes grew to the size of dinner plates and he exclaimed, "Hey, what is *that?*"

"It's uh, well it's an official NASA lunchbox," he said. He glanced up at me and I swore I caught a slight blush move across his cheeks.

"*What?*" Cole exclaimed and clambered onto the couch to sit beside him. "That is *so cool.*"

"Cole, Shawn is on his break." I frowned, but couldn't help appreciate the extra time this was buying me with the nurse.

"Mm, no, it's fine," Shawn replied as he placed his sandwich down onto a small plate before wiping his fingers with a cloth napkin. He smiled at Cole. "Do you like NASA?"

"Hm, well… I like *space,*" Cole said, his eyes fixed on the lunchbox.

"Really?" Shawn asked, his eyebrows raising. I caught more than a hint of excitement in his voice.

"Uh, yeah, I'm a total space *nut,*" Cole said before running his mouth off. "And not just like, the *moon* like other stupid—"

"Cole," I warned him.

"I like the planets, but also outer galaxies and I'd *love* to see a blackhole one day," he said while I watched Shawn's face, his eyes set on Cole and his head nodding in agreement. "Dad got me a telescope but I'm not great at using it yet."

"Well, it sounds like you've got a very nice dad," Shawn said, and I caught his eye for a second before he looked back at Cole.

"How'd you get an official lunchbox?" I asked, in a not so subtle way of inserting myself into the conversation.

"I won it, actually," Shawn said. Again his eyes met mine, and I was struck dumb. They were the most unusual hazel I'd ever seen. Green and gold flecks were interspersed with what I could only describe as silver, and if I looked closely, I could almost say I was spotting stars in his eyes. Galaxies. Funny, considering the conversation he was having with Cole.

"How?" Liam asked, shyly moving over to the couch and looking at the lunchbox in question.

"Oh," Shawn said, and then started laughing nervously. "It was from a dog show, actually."

"You have a *dog*?" Cole bounced excitedly on the couch.

"A show dog?" I asked.

"Yes and no. It was just a silly little dog trick contest. LuLu isn't show material, not like some of the dogs who win blue ribbon prizes, but she knows how to do some cool tricks." Shawn smiled, and Cole stared at him like he was talking nonsense.

"Do you have to walk your dog *all* the time?" Cole asked. "Mom makes me walk Paco *all* the time."

Shawn chuckled and shook his head. "How big is Paco?"

"He's *huge*," Liam interjected.

"Yeah, he's huge," Cole said.

"He's a medium husky," I remarked to clarify.

"Ah. Well, he probably needs more walks than my LuLu does. She's a corgi, so she only needs a short walk in the afternoons when I get off my shift. She loves the dog park, though."

"Paco hates the dog park," Cole announced. "We just let him out into the woods and sometimes he runs with us on the full moon and—"

"No he doesn't," I said with a warm smile, annoyed I'd now have to steer Cole away from saying something about shifters. Usually the best way to do that was to distract him with something else. "Cole, we need to take this food to Bryce before he starves to death. Shawn, it was nice to meet you."

"Nice to meet you," Cole and Liam repeated as they hurried out of the room.

"Maybe we'll see you later," I said to Shawn, feeling completely defeated by the sudden ending to our conversation, but I didn't really have any real choice if I didn't want to take the risk of Cole blurting out the truth of our existence. That was one of the issues in a shifter finding a mate in a human; it was having to explain about shifters and mates and knotting… I swallowed at the thought of knotting Shawn, feeling my skin heat.

"I hope so," he said with a small smile, his gaze still focused on me. I gave him a stiff grin and forced myself to walk away.

"You're *welcome*," Cole said as I met up with him in the hallway.

"For what?" I asked, handing him one of the bags of crisps and giving the other to Liam.

"For getting the *intel*," Liam said.

"For getting you the *hookup*," Cole said as he ripped open his bag.

"What the heck are you talking about?" I was not in the mood for their cheer. "Where did you hear about *intel*?"

"Jaxon," they said in unison.

"He told us to follow you and get the nurse guy talking about himself," Cole said.

I grumbled and silently cursed Jaxon for assuming that *I* needed help from a couple of eight year-olds.

"Well, thanks." I sighed as we rounded the hall toward Bryce's room, but I had to admit I hadn't gotten any information out of Shawn myself, while Cole had discovered some key *intel* that he likes space, and has a dog that he walks every afternoon…

Suddenly, it dawned on me. I grabbed my phone and dialed Nicole's number.

She answered after one ring. "'Sup?"

"I need to borrow Paco."

***

"Oh my god, is that LuLu?" Cole asked as we drew closer to the dog park. Paco strained on his lead and threatened to pull the kid flat onto his face as we got close to the fence. My wolf started tugging just as hard as soon as my eyes locked onto Shawn who was throwing a toy for his brown and white corgi on the other side of the park.

"She's *so short*," Liam said, giggling while opening the dog park gate. Paco shot forward, and Cole let out a yelp as his arm was practically ripped out of its socket.

"Paco, sit," I growled low and menacing. The dog immediately cowered and sat down with his head bowed. I was pleased that a real alpha growl still had some power. Cole rubbed his shoulder and handed me the leash. I unclipped Paco who looked up at me with a cautious expression in his bright blue eyes until I nodded, and then he immediately dashed across the grass. I looked up and grinned as I watched Paco sprint straight for LuLu.

"Paco has a crush on LuLu," Cole said.

I noticed Shawn look up in surprise at the sight of our pure white husky approaching his corgi, and then relaxed as LuLu reacted with excitement. Shawn glanced over at us, probably to check out the owner of the husky, and I caught another look of surprise as he recognized me. I took a deep breath and caught a hint of his scent on the breeze. I let out a pleased moan and made my way over to him.

"Hey," I said, laughing. "Twice in one day!"

"Hi there. "What a coincidence."

"Crazy, huh? It's Shawn, right?" I asked, as if I could forget.

"Right." He nodded, a shy smile spreading across his face. "And you're…Linc?"

"Yes. And this is Paco."

"The infamous Paco." Shawn watched as the husky licked LuLu's face. "Uh, well, this is LuLu."

"Hi, LuLu!" Cole and Liam said way too loudly as they started playing with the two dogs, distracting them from annoying Shawn and me. I had to admit—the kids were proving to be good wingmen.

"So, nice park," I said, and then grimaced at my own awkwardness. I licked my lips and wondered what the hell I was thinking, turning up here like this. This was maybe my second time in the dog park—for good reason. Apart from Paco and LuLu, every dog in the place was on high alert, ears raised and eyes looking at me, waiting for some kind of command. I just prayed that Shawn wouldn't notice.

"It's not bad," he said, and then sighed. "Well... I'm kind of sick of it, honestly."

"Oh?" I asked.

"Hm, we walk here every day. I think LuLu still likes it, but I could use some variety."

"Huh... You ever go hiking in the woods with her?" I asked, scratching my head.

"The *woods*?" Shawn raised his eyebrows. "With that little bear-snack? I don't think so."

I laughed and shook my head. "Well if you ever want to come with us, I'm sure Paco would protect her."

"And what about me?"

I glanced at Shawn and caught a glimmer of cheekiness in his eye.

"Oh, I'd be happy to protect you." I smiled and watched as Shawn struggled to meet my eyes. That got his attention. "So, we're going to grab some pizza later, would you like to join us?" I asked, crossing my fingers.

Shawn didn't react. He was non-expressively gazing at LuLu who was romping around the park with Paco chasing her, and the kids chasing after him. I didn't know whether to repeat myself or change the subject when he cleared his throat. I waited for a moment, but there was still no answer. Oh geez, had I scared him off already?

"Not a date," I said, if that was what he was worried about. "Just hanging out with me and the boys. Sorry, I should have said that in the first place. Just... It's nice to meet someone new who has an interest in dogs and...space."

"You're into space?" he asked.

"Well, I'm trying to be," I said. "Cole's obsessed and I don't want to get left behind. He'll be talking about quasars and interstellar light waves, and I'll just be sitting there wondering when my eight-year-old became smarter than me."

To my surprise, Shawn let out a laugh before he quickly regained his composure.

"I could point you in the right direction. Some online tutorials, some cool videos. Enough to get you speaking the same language, at least."

"Well, that'd be great," I said, genuinely appreciative for his offer.

"How about tonight?"

I raised my eyebrows and a sly grin spread across his face.

"Maybe over pizza?" he added.

"Hm..." I pretended to consider his offer. I looked up at the sky and pursed my lips until he laughed and playfully slapped my stomach with the back of his hand.

"Very funny," he said sarcastically.

I smiled at him, but the contact had sent a thrill all over my body and I still felt it reverberating through me. "Can we pick you up at seven?"

"Make it six." He smiled warmly. "I have an early shift tomorrow, and I need my beauty sleep."

***

"Ew!" Cole exclaimed from the backseat, quickly cranking down the back window.

"Paco farted," Liam complained as he covered his nose with his jacket.

"Remind me to spray some air freshener in here before we pick up Shawn," I mumbled, bracing myself against the cold wind that rushed through the car.

"Hey, Dad," Cole said quietly as I drove us up to Nicole's driveway.

"Yeah, buddy?"

"Remember to spray some air freshener in here before we pick up Shawn!" Cole fell about laughing, and I rolled my eyes, wondering if there was ever going to be a moment of genuine emotion between us again, now he was growing into a rambunctious pre-teen.

"Thanks, Cole," I replied, deadpan, as I shut off the car. We tumbled out and the boys ran into the house with Paco on their heels and me not far behind. I found Nicole in the kitchen, brewing up a pot of stew.

"Did he do the job?" she asked without taking her eyes off the pot.

"Who?"

"Paco—did he land you the date?"

"I think... Yeah... I think he did," I said, sighing and resting my head in my hands as I stood at the kitchen island.

Nicole spun around and squinted at me. "You *think*? Are you going on a date or not?"

"Well... We're going for pizza at Tony's tonight."

"*Oooh.*"

"But I'm taking the boys with me..."

"Excuse me? Come again?" She craned her head as though she hadn't heard.

"I mean, if you're fine with me taking our son to hang out with a guy you've never met," I said.

"Please, it's fine, you know I trust you completely. But uh... Just one question... What the hell were you thinking? Cole's a cool kid, but he's doesn't exactly set the mood for romance." She lowered the spoon in her hand in disappointment.

"I was thinking about how I could get this incredible guy who I've just met to hang out with me, and how I could get him to think I'm a normal person and not a creepy stalker."

"He's a human, huh?"

"Yeah." I grabbed a stick of celery off the counter and took a bite out of it.

"And you're *sure* he's your fated mate?" she asked quietly, glancing around to make sure Cole was out of earshot.

"Certain. Completely. The way he *smells* is one thing, but when we touched..." I sighed again and took another bite as I gazed sadly at the island. Nicole let out a high-pitched noise and I looked up to find her face squeezed up in an excited expression, like she was about to burst.

"Fated love!" She clapped her hands excitedly, sending a spray of soup off the spoon all across the kitchen. I laughed and scooped up a dollop that had landed on the counter in front of me.

"Yes, and I'm still in shock. I can't believe this is happening to me at last. But how am I supposed to show *him* that we're fated? Humans don't get the whole fated mate thing, they just have relationships. There's no real magic involved, no absolutes. They don't know that for a shifter to find his fated mate is to love forever." I sighed, then moaned as the flavor of oregano and bay leaf hit my tongue. "Damn, this is a good stew."

"Too bad you're having *pizza*, or I'd invite you to stay for dinner." Nicole grinned then turned back to stir the pot.

"Oh shit, did you make this for the boys? Sorry. I should have asked you about dinner plans before I set up the date, but I didn't know I was going to drag them along with me."

Nicole shook her head. "Don't be silly, the stew won't go to waste. I'll take some to the hospital before the run tonight. Bryce has been complaining about the sandwiches…"

***

After herding the boys back into the truck, we drove to my place and got ready. While the kids were upstairs fighting over whether to wear identical or complementary t-shirts, I stepped out into the cold to call Jaxon. I filled him in on the plan and asked if it was fine to take Liam. Another thing I should have done first, but how was I to know Shawn wouldn't accept my invitation without the boys as a buffer.

"Of course. Cute idea for a date. And we really appreciate you taking care of him while Bryce is in hospital," he said.

The sun was setting and I paced up and down my porch to keep warm. I realized I hadn't told him anything more about Shawn being my fated mate. Everyone in the hospital room had known there was something going on, but I hadn't confirmed the extent of who Shawn was to me. It was an odd thing to keep from my alpha pack leader, and I decided it was because I was more than a little nervous about blowing it.

"Is everything still good there? Lori sleeping?" I asked, changing the subject.

"Yep, she's resting up and so is Bryce. The two of them are dozing in and out, and to be honest, so am I. It's the most relaxed I've felt in a long time."

I laughed. "Like a resort, huh?"

"Yeah. Have a great night. Take it slow if you can manage it, but remember, he's human. Make sure to keep the boys from spilling every secret about the pack."

"God knows I'll try."

***

Shawn's place was in town, across from the dog park, and I followed the directions he'd given me but still managed to get lost on the way.

"Number *ten*!" Cole yelled from the backseat when we drove past for the second time.

"Are you excited we're have dinner with Shawn?" I asked tentatively as I parked just down the block from the terrace house at number ten.

"Yeah!" they said in unison, and then Cole added, "We're getting pizza, right?"

I chuckled and nodded. "Yes, we're getting pizza. And what are the rules at Tony's Pizza?"

"Eat all the pizza," Liam said, setting Cole off into a set of giggles.

"Talk loudly about *wolves*!" Cole cried.

"No, eat pizza, howl and *shift* into wolves." Liam also collapsed into a fit of giggles, and then both of them were laughing so hard I thought I might have to turn around and take them both home.

By the time I'd calmed them down and reminded them of the *real* rules, Shawn was standing outside his house, glancing down the street nervously. My stomach tightened and my heart fluttered. I felt my wolf whimpering and yearning to get closer to him, so I gave him what he wanted.

Chapter 4 - Shawn

Standing at the front of my yard, I glanced down Pack Lane, looking for any sign of them. It was already dark out, but the street lights shone on a truck parked just down the block. Realizing it might be him, I felt anxiety kick in all over again. I sighed, trying to ignore the equal measure of excitement and nervousness making my hands shake. I'd already gone through a bout of nerves earlier while getting dressed.

I'd never had an alpha pursue me so quickly and aggressively as Linc. Normally if someone *happened* to see me twice in one day, I'd think they just had full moon fever and wanted to have some quick sex. Which I actually wouldn't mind, if I was being honest. Linc was hot. I loved his dark hair and short crew cut, his striking jaw that gave him an air of rugged masculinity. He was brawny with huge biceps and had a set of wide shoulders that could possibly carry a Great Dane in an emergency.

His unambiguous desire to get to know me was a little intimidating, but only because it felt there was more going on than appeared on the surface. For a start, I'd wondered why he invited me out with two little kids because that was the quickest way to cockblock himself, if all he was after was sex. However, if he was after more... I let out a sigh and scolded myself for overthinking things, and for putting high expectations on the night.

The door of the truck opened, and out stepped Linc. I took a deep breath as my heart started jackhammering and I felt myself getting *way* too enthusiastic for a not-date. He spotted me and smiled, waving and making his way up the street.

"Play it *cool*," I mumbled to myself as I wrapped my scarf tightly around my neck and walked toward him.

"Hey." He smiled warmly as he brought me into a hug. "Nice to see you."

"Mm, you too," I replied, lingering a little too long as I enjoyed the feel of his strong arms around me.

"Ready to help these kids eat way too much pizza?" he asked, offering me his arm. I hesitated for just a moment. It was an old-fashioned gesture, and this combination of his chivalry, straightforwardness and family-oriented approach was a heady mix. He definitely seemed like the single-minded type, even more so than most alphas I knew. Something I found incredibly sexy.

I took a deep breath and nodded, and then slipped my arm in his, letting him lead me to his truck. I wasn't surprised when he held open the door for me.

"Hi boys," I said, smiling at the kids in the backseat. "What are you gonna get at Tony's?"

"Lots of pizza," Cole replied, grabbing at his face and acting like it was being eaten by a monster.

"*One* pizza," Linc insisted as he jumped into the truck and turned on the engine.

"One pizza," Cole and Liam responded together sadly.

As I buckled up, I stole a glance at Linc and felt myself being drawn to him even more than before. I guess I should have been a little more guarded because I knew running into him at the park couldn't have been an accident. It seemed perhaps *too* intentional, but right then I decided I didn't care.

***

When we got to Tony's Pizza, Linc held the door for me again, and he even pulled out a chair for me when we got to the table. I could tell he wanted to ensure I was enjoying myself, which helped me relax even more. Plus I felt more than a little flattered by his attention. Toward the end of my relationship with Phillip, he wouldn't even say "good morning" to me, let alone do little things to make me feel desired. Then he dumped me as unceremoniously as a bowl of leftovers he had forgotten in the back of the fridge.

I took a deep breath and focused on the menu and the conversation going on around me, instead of delving deep into my traumatic past.

"Do you like olives?" Cole asked, swinging his legs under the table as he looked at the menu.

"I *love* olives," I replied.

"Do you like *peppers*?" Liam asked in a quieter voice.

"I *love* peppers," I said, giving him a warm smile. I caught Linc's eye and saw that he was practically beaming at me. I looked away quickly and tried to ignore how excited it had made me feel.

"Olive and pepper pizza please!" Cole cried out, a little too loudly.

"Shh." Linc scolded him, and his son made a theatrical show of zipping his lip. I couldn't help but let out a chuckle and gave Linc an apologetic smile.

"Can we have garlic bread?" Cole asked me.

"Uh, better ask your dad," I said, diverting to the man in charge.

"One large pie will be enough for us, kiddo," Linc said.

"*Please*, Dad."

"If you're still hungry after the pizza, we'll get some," he declared.

"Dad! Please!".

Linc looked at me, exasperated, and I guessed that in any other circumstances Linc wouldn't have allowed his son to act that way, but he didn't want to cause a scene.

"Hey, Cole, have you ever seen a meteor through your telescope?" I asked, not quite believing the diversion tactic would work. But it did—like a charm. Cole sat upright and looked at me with wide eyes.

"No! Have you? Really?" he asked, his jaw practically on the floor.

"I sure have. Completely by accident, of course. I was looking at Saturn when it came zooming past. Just incredible. We're pretty lucky to see so many stars around here."

"Yeah, and I can see even more now because I have a real telescope," Cole said.

"That's cool! What do you see through the telescope?"

"Lots of stuff. I have an astronomy coloring book, so I'm working my way through its pages and trying to find all the stars in the book. Last night I saw Orion, and the Big Dipper, and the Little Dipper!"

"I like looking for constellations too."

"Really?"

"Mm. I have a telescope that can take photos. Would you like to see some photos I took last week?"

"Yeah!" Cole said, scooting his chair closer to me and leaning over to look at my phone as I opened my album of stargazing photos. As I swiped through some photos of the constellations I saw during a clear night the week before, Linc and Liam leaned over the table to also get a look.

"Wow, those are really hi-def photos!" Liam exclaimed.

"He can take photos with his telescope!" Cole explained.

"That's pretty neat," Liam said as I zoomed in on a photo of Venus. "It looks like a star... But it's a planet?"

"Yeah, sometimes it shines really bright, but if you look closer you can see that it's got a blue tinge to it. I took that photo from the beach. There's less light pollution down there so it's a great spot for stargazing."

"That's so cool. I wish I had a telescope like that," Cole said, sounding a little forlorn.

"Well, maybe next time I'm going down to the beach you guys can come meet me and try it out," I offered.

"Really?" Cole asked with the biggest smile I'd ever seen. It was like Christmas had come early.

"Yeah, of course," I said, then glanced at Linc to gauge whether I'd gone too far with the introduction. I was shocked to find that he was beaming at me, just as enraptured as the kids were.

"Well, when is the next time you're going?" he asked.

"Yeah, when?" Cole demanded.

"I don't know yet. It depends on the weather and my work schedule. Sometimes I have to work night shifts at the hospital."

"That *stinks*," Cole said, looking back at the photo of Venus with more than a little disappointment.

"Cole, Shawn has a very important job. Sometimes babies are born at night. Nothing can be done about it."

"Hmph," Cole replied.

"It does kind of stink," I agreed. "But like your dad said, it has to be done. No two ways about it."

A waiter brought our pizza over and we all grabbed a slice. As I was trying to disentangle my slice from a molten web of stringy cheese, I glanced at Linc and realizing I didn't know much about him.

"What do you do for work, Linc?" I asked, hungrily feasting on his amazing bone structure and toffee-colored eyes as he turned his head to look at me. His radiant smile widened more than I thought appropriate for the mundane question I'd asked, but I had to admit, his smile was pretty stunning.

"Construction," Linc said. "I'm the site manager for a project over on Growling Oak Way right now. It's a major renovation, so it should keep me busy through next year. Gets a little quiet over Christmas, but there are plenty of odd jobs around town."

That explains the giant muscles and machismo.

"Is it a far commute for you?" I asked.

"Nah, I live on the grounds of the uh, the Country Club," he said, hesitating just a bit.

"We do too," Cole added.

"I've never been there. I hear it's kind of...nice." Actually, I heard only the richest people in town lived there. It was an exclusive gated community.

"Well, it's just where we live. Our whole pa—uh…family lives there. You should come up one day to check out my telescope," Cole suggested. "It's not as high-tech as yours but I know a good spot for stargazing too. There's a place up in the woods."

"That sounds great, I'd love to," I said, smiling at him. He was a nice kid, if a little cocky. "We'll have to get some other adults to come with us, though. I might get scared being in the woods just the two of us! Hey, are any of you gonna go out and look at the full moon tonight?"

"Oh yeah, we *always* go out on the full moon," Cole said, then broke into a fit of giggles.

"Why's that?" I asked.

"It's a, uh, kind of family tradition," Linc explained, darting his eyes over to the boys.

"Huh. Interesting. Are your families ritualists or something?" I asked.

"Not exactly…" Linc shook his head as the boys started giggling again.

"Well, I've heard rumors about wolves on your side of town. I've never actually seen them myself but apparently there's a few of them. Or so my friend Trevor says, anyway."

Cole and Liam broke down giggling.

"I've heard those rumors, too," Linc replied, rubbing the back of his neck with visible agitation.

"Wolves *looooove* the full moon," Liam said with a mouthful of pizza, almost choking on the last few words and falling off his seat as he started laughing even harder. Linc shot him a look.

"Chew your food, please," Linc said in a stern, fatherly voice. Warmth flooded my chest as I saw him gaze at Liam with an expression at once adoring and concerned. Linc's paternal instincts, even to a child who wasn't his, were very attractive, and I couldn't help but feel that familiar longing to be a father. I tamped it down because now wasn't the time to be envious.

"So, be careful out there when you're looking at the moon," I said.

"We, uh… We will," Linc said, giving me a sweet smile.

"Maybe you could bring Paco out with you. But… Would he even protect you against a wolf?"

Now it was Linc's turn to burst out laughing, the deep timbre incredibly sexy. I watched with amusement as he wiped a tear from his eye and collected himself.

"Paco would probably think a wolf was his friend," Linc said with a smirk. "I don't know if his loyalty to humans runs that deep."

"Well, I'd offer up LuLu but she'd be even more useless," I said with a laugh.

"Yeah, I think she'd be more of a liability in that situation," Linc said, laughing along with me.

"She's so little!" Liam stated. "She probably can't even run very fast on her tiny legs!"

"You'd be surprised. I bet if she saw a wolf she'd run so fast in the opposite direction you wouldn't know where she went."

All of the sudden, Liam let out a shout. "Ouch! You butthead!"

"What's the problem?" Linc asked him.

"Cole pinched my arm, and it really hurt!"

"You started it!" Cole shouted back at Liam.

"Okay, cranky boys. *Enough*. Nicole should be here to pick you up any minute. Does anyone need the bathroom?" Linc asked.

"Yes," both boys said simultaneously, pouting at Linc.

"Okay, go take care of that now so you're ready to go when Nicole pulls up, please."

"*You* started it," Liam grumbled back at Cole as they stalked off to the back of the restaurant.

"Behave yourselves in there!" Linc called after them. Then he sighed and turned to me.

"Sorry about that," he said with a smile. He took a sip of his soda, never breaking eye contact with me.

"It's fine, I deal with kids all day long. Younger ones, but still... Same screaming," I said, smiling back at him and meeting his gaze. "I'm impressed two boys their age lasted this long without a meltdown."

"Actually, they usually get along great. Nicole is uh, Cole's mom. We were only together for a brief...time. Good friends now, though."

A moment of silence hung between us. Gazing into his eyes, I felt an undeniable connection with him. My heart felt tingly and a rush of lust flooded my veins. My breath caught, but I reminded myself this wasn't necessarily going to go anywhere, and if it did, it might not last. I pulled my focus away from Linc's enticing eyes to look out the window of the pizzeria. Sparse raindrops were streaking the window and the wind seemed to be picking up.

"The weather doesn't seem ideal for your full moon festivities," I said quietly.

Linc cracked his knuckles and pulled out his cell phone. "Yeah, it's only supposed to last another hour." He read the forecast off his phone, then he put it down and looked up to meet my gaze again. "After the boys have left, I'll drive you home."

He looked so intently into my eyes it seemed he was trying to read my mind. I hadn't expected him to take me home without the boys. That kind of went beyond a not-date, but I was so curious to see what would happen if we had some time alone that I agreed.

"That would be nice, thank you," I said.

A blue SUV pulled up just as the boys were coming back from the bathroom. The driver waved through the windshield and Linc waved back through the pizzeria window.

"There's my mom!" Cole said, nudging Liam's elbow as they came up to the table.

"Thanks for pizza, Linc," Liam said politely.

"Sure thing, buddy." Linc ruffled Liam's hair, and then kissed Cole on his head.

"I'll see you later, boys," Linc said as the kids scampered out the door and into Nicole's waiting car. Linc paid the bill, then we headed out to his truck.

"Thank you for bringing me here. It was nice. Cole and Liam are great kids," I said as he pulled open the door for me.

"Well, Cole can be a little...enthusiastic, especially when talking about stargazing, so thank you for sharing your interest with him. Just to let you know, I've liked your company too." Linc's warm smile started butterflies in my stomach, and I found myself dreading saying goodbye. I didn't want the night to end. Linc's mysterious intensity had me dying to know more about him, and I wondered if I should invite him inside when we got to my place.

What is going on with me? I just met this guy. Don't get carried away. He doesn't know everything *about you and might not like want you once he finds out.*

Still... I wanted to see what might happen between us, and I'd made a decision to invite him when we pulled up to the front of the house.

Linc turned to look at me. "Let me walk you to your door?"

"Sure, if you don't mind getting a little wet," I said, smirking at the slight innuendo, surprised a little at my audacity. I wasn't used to making advances, even subtle ones.

"Not at all," Linc said, his own smirk growing into a grin as he got out of the truck to open my door for me again.

At my front stoop I noticed a few raindrops caught on the stubble on Linc's upper lip. I felt a longing in my heart as I got carried away imagining what it would like to kiss a handsome, burly alpha who was already such a father figure. He seemed to notice me looking and smiled.

"Could I get your number?" he asked sweetly.

I nodded, and he handed me his phone. As I took it from him, my fingers grazed his and I felt something like an electric spark jump between us, as if I'd been rubbing a fleece blanket on the way over. I shivered, then laughed self-consciously.

"Are you cold?" Linc asked, warm concern darting across his face.

"No, you shocked me. Didn't you feel that?"

"Oh yeah, I did. I didn't realize you felt it too." He looked down and pushed his hands into his coat pockets. The moment of slight awkwardness made the longing in my chest grow stronger. My body was aching to touch him, and the feeling grew stronger by the millisecond. I made a split-second decision and leaned in to kiss his cheek. Just a friendly, appreciative gesture. It didn't have to be serious right away... But he looked up at the exact moment.

"Well, have a nice night..."

His sudden movement meant my kiss landed slightly off my original target. My lips made contact with the edge of his mouth, and his lips parted in surprise as I pulled away. We stared at each other for a moment. Desire churned even stronger in my stomach—like a washing machine that had reached the spin cycle. The scent of his cologne filled my nose, peppered and spiced like a strong dark rum. There was something else too, musky and feral. Before I knew it, I heard myself saying, "Want to come in for a drink or a...coffee, maybe?"

Linc's eyes brightened. "Yeah, I do."

As soon as I pushed the door open, LuLu bounced up and down in the doorway, almost pushing herself through the opening and onto the street.

"Hi baby!" She licked my hands enthusiastically.

"Hello again, LuLu," Linc said, reaching down so she could sniff his hands once we were inside. She ran full-speed across the kitchen in the opposite direction, slipping slightly on the kitchen tiles, and disappeared into the living room.

Linc laughed awkwardly. "What did I do?"

"Beats me," I said with a shrug. "Maybe she doesn't like your cologne."

"Hm. I hope that's not it. That stuff is expensive."

"Don't take it personally. She's a fussy princess. Anyway, I think the smell suits you. Can I take your coat?"

Linc unzipped his black wool coat. I enjoyed the sight of him shrugging it off his massive shoulders. As I reached to hang Linc's coat on a hook by the door, LuLu came bounding back into the room with her red and white rope toy in her mouth.

"Oh, I see," Linc said, grinning as he gripped the rope. "Play time, is it?"

LuLu started growling and tugging on the rope with all her might.

"You're tough for such a little dog." Linc mercifully let her gain some traction considering one of his arms was the size of her whole body.

"What can I offer you? Coffee? Wine? Beer?" I asked, wiggling out of my own coat. I noticed Linc's eyes narrow as he watched me. I turned around, secretly hoping he would be checking out my ass as I hung my coat up. My tight jeans would have given him a pretty clear view of what I was working with.

"A beer would be great."

I pulled two beers out of the fridge, and then opened a drawer to look for a bottle opener. As I rummaged around I realized how much being here with him and LuLu playing happily was nice. Really nice. Then I remembered; if this got anywhere near serious I'd have to tell him about being infertile. If he was looking for someone to have a new family with, then I was unfairly leading him on if I didn't let him know.

Then again, he already has a son. Maybe he doesn't want any more kids.

Finally finding the bottle opener I slid the drawer closed. I shouldn't be thinking that far ahead, but I really liked him. I sighed. I needed to take a step back and just enjoy the vibe we had going on right now. With that in mind I opened the beers, but when I spun around, I saw Linc standing next to me. Searching his eyes for what felt like the millionth time that day, I felt time slip away. It felt like I was moving through molasses as I ever so slowly handed him the bottle.

Once he had it in his hand, Linc raised his bottle to toast. I brought my bottle up to his and our knuckles grazed. "What are we toasting to?" I asked.

"Hmm... To the full moon?"

"Yes. Complete madness. I'll drink to that," I said, smiling and holding eye contact as I took a sip. I wanted to get closer to him, breathe in his scent. "Do you want to sit down?" I suggested.

Linc nodded and made a beeline for the living room. He beat me to the couch and plopped down on it, placing his beer bottle on the coffee table. I sat next to him and angled myself so I could look at him, without being too far away. It felt like he had a glow surrounding him, and I wanted to be in it.

"You were really good with the Cole and Liam. I should have warned you about them being terrors sometimes. It's a tricky age." He picked at the label on his beer. "And, you know. Not everyone likes kids."

I swallowed nervously. It felt like he'd said it as bait. I guessed it mattered to him that I was fond of kids, especially his son. "Oh, I like kids. I like them a lot." I left it at that, but I could hear the sadness in my voice and I'd be shocked if Linc hadn't heard it too.

"That's nice to know. Either way, I'd love to see you again soon," Linc said. "Without the kids."

"Um, are you sure? Because Cole *really* wants to see my telescope," I said, poking fun at him.

"I know, and I'm sure he'll get his chance. But yeah, I'd like to just...spend some time getting to know you better. If you want that," he said quietly.

"Yeah, that would be nice."

"So how about a real date on Friday night?"

"I work the evening shift on Friday, but I'm free after that. I get off at nine, so if that's not too late I can meet you then?"

"Nine is perfectly fine," Linc said.

Silence fell between us. Not tense, but there was something in the air that had me swallowing hard.

"Can I kiss you?" Linc suddenly asked, his eyelids looking heavy as his dark lashes swept downward. He was looking longingly at my lips. He was asking with blunt confidence, but he was at least polite enough to ask rather than just lean in. And if I was honest, he was just too sexy for me to resist.

I didn't waste any time on answering his question. I just leaned forward and planted my lips on him. It felt amazingly good, so different to the accidental peck I had pulled off on my doorstep. This time I could take my time, pay attention, and enjoy. And I did.

He pressed his lips to mine with considerable force, as if he'd been holding back a long time from doing just that. The firmness of his kiss wasn't too surprising, but when he put one of his big hands on my shoulder and pulled me closer, he did so gently. He parted his lips and caressed the seam of mine with the tip of his tongue, sending a tingle straight to my cock. I moaned and inhaled sharply through my nose. Linc nibbled at my lower lip briefly, then pulled back and took a deep breath. He stared at me, his eyes blown wide with lust, which I was sure mirrored my own. I wanted him to kiss me again, to pull me onto his lap, hold me, caress me. Instead, Linc shook his head.

"I better get going. With you having an early shift tomorrow and all."

A little shocked and a lot disappointed, I blinked at him. He'd been following me like a scent hound all day, and he had me willing in his arms. Why stop now? Maybe he didn't like the way I kissed. I didn't think I was that bad, but I had been out of practice for some time. Unless his leaving was his way of showing amazing will power.

"Okay," I said, not sure what else I could say.

"Thanks for the drink, Shawn," he said, standing up.

"I'll see you on Friday?" I hated that I made it sound like a question, but I didn't know what was going through Linc's mind.

"Friday," he repeated with a smile. "I'll be looking forward to that for the rest of the week."

My heart surged in both relief and joy that he still wanted to see me. I grinned like an idiot, and then walked him to the door. I handed him his coat, and pressed one more passionate kiss on his lips before he left.

I watched Linc walk to his truck and felt an odd tugging in my chest, as if something had caught around my heart—and the farther he walked away, the stronger the tug. It felt like he was wrapping up my heart and taking it with him.

Chapter 5 - Linc

The clouds had moved over the sky by the time I stepped outside and the full moon lit up Pack Lane and the dog park across the way. The light reflected brightly from the puddles the rain had left, and I wondered if they'd freeze overnight. I pulled my jacket tight across my chest and turned back to take one final glance at Shawn as he held the door open.

The kiss he'd given me still lingered on my lips, and just like the first kiss in his living room I'd felt a warm tingle warm me from the inside out. I took that warmth with me as I walked down his driveway, my wolf whining and pawing at my chest, begging me to stay with Shawn, even as it wanted to run under the moon. The feeling of Shawn's mouth against mine had already become addictive, and it had taken all of my willpower to pull away. I wished I could spend the night melting into his kiss, but there was somewhere I needed to be.

***

I drove straight up Pack Lane from Shawn's house and felt the blood in my veins pumping a little harder and faster as I neared the homestead. The full moon was pulling on me just as hard as my connection with Shawn had tugged at me earlier.

The gates to the homestead opened as I approached, and as I drove up to Wolf Lodge I wondered if I really would be able to bring Shawn into this world with me one day. A human amongst shifters was often a tricky combination. Though I knew Jaxon had managed it with Bryce, it didn't always go to plan.

The pack was amassed on the grounds around the Lodge that sat in the middle of our homestead. The Lodge was a large building just inside the gates at the end of Pack Lane, though on the other side of town to where Shawn lived, and looked like any other country club from the outside. The full moon lit the manicured lawns, tall oaks, and the ponds that decorated the Lodge's grounds. I parked nearby and hurried over to the group, not wanting to miss the run.

I spotted Nicole talking with her brother, Gavin Stanton, while Cole and Liam played with their friends and Paco nearby. Nicole waved when I caught her eye. Gavin turned and gave me a huge smile when he spotted me.

"Hey, brother," he said, pulling me into a hug. He was a big guy and used his brawn to work as a bodyguard and protector around the homestead, but his hugs were the sweetest I'd ever had. I gave him a squeeze and a firm slap on the back.

"Hey, Gav. Hey, Nic," I said to Nicole over Gavin's shoulder.

"Hi there, Lothario," she said, attempting a joke as Gavin freed me. "How'd the date go?"

"Ah, I don't know, good I think," I said, rubbing the back of my neck. "I'm kind of still buzzing from it. We—"

"Shifters!" Jaxon's booming voice came from the top of the stairs leading up to the Lodge.

"We'll catch up after, okay?" Nicole whispered, and I nodded before I turned my attention to Jaxon. All eyes were on him as he stood topless in front of the Lodge, his muscles bulging under the power of the full moon.

"Tonight we run as a pack knowing our numbers are growing," Jaxon announced. He caught my gaze and I swore I saw a flicker of something sly pass across his eyes. Was he talking about *me*? No, surely not so soon—I'd literally just met Shawn and had no idea how to even *broach* the topic of shifters with him, let alone bring him into the pack.

Jaxon grinned. "My baby daughter was born today. Lori is the newest member of our pack. As many of you know, Bryce is still in the hospital—please keep your pack brother in your hearts as we run, I know he truly wishes he could be out in the woods with us tonight."

Applause moved through the crowd as Jaxon smiled proudly. I told myself to relax—of course he was talking about Lori, not Shawn... I was getting carried away.

"To Lori!" someone shouted, and a loud cheer broke out through the pack.

Jaxon looked the proudest I'd ever seen him. Soon enough, he tilted his head back and let out a blood-curdling howl. The sound of it shot through me and pulled hard on every inch of my skin. My wolf ran in circles in my chest, stirring up excitement inside me.

Cole rushed over and wrapped an arm around my leg, and Liam raced over just behind him.

"Feeling alright, Liam?" Nicole asked, checking on Jaxon's adopted son. Liam was actually Bryce's nephew, and had been born a human. He'd only been turned into a shifter by Jaxon a few months earlier, and last night was the first time Liam had shifted. He didn't seem to have any trouble this morning, but tonight would be the first time he did so with the pack, so maybe he was nervous over that.

"I think so," he said, putting on a brave face.

"Just focus on the feeling here," Gavin said, pointing to the center of his own chest. "Follow it, let it lead you. Close your eyes if you have to."

"Good advice," I agreed, and ruffled Liam's hair. "Don't worry, Liam. You're a natural."

"What about me?" Cole asked.

"You're *literally* a natural. You were born a cub, so you've never had to really learn how to shift," Nicole said.

Suddenly, Jaxon let out another howl. This one was higher, louder, and even more resonant. I looked over and found that he'd shifted into his wolf form. Seeing my alpha's wolf always touched on something deep and ancient inside me—a feeling of familiarity, admiration, and *need*. I couldn't hold back any longer. I glanced at Cole and Liam, who had their eyes closed, to make sure they were ready. I let myself shift.

Immediately, my senses were sharpened. My ears perked up as other pack members shifted and joined in the howl. Cole shifted, and Liam quickly followed with no signs of discomfort or struggle. I felt a surge of pride and I nudged my snout against both of them to let them know.

Jaxon looked across his pack and met my eyes. I was his right-hand man within the pack, so I trotted up to stand beside my best friend. However, that's when I felt a tinge of sadness radiating off him. I glanced at him and he lowered his head. I immediately knew he missed Bryce and wished his mate and his newborn were here so he could protect them.

I gave Jaxon a reassuring nudge before I turned to the pack and let out a short bark. Everyone's attention fell on us. Jaxon burst forward and sprinted through the pack toward the woods that surrounded our homestead. A flurry of paws hit the ground as we took off, following him into the night.

I loved the way the scents changed as I broke through the tree line. The air went from smelling like freshly mowed grass to wet moss, fertile dirt, and rotting leaves. My paws kicked up the odor of mud and bugs as I ran through the forest, chasing Jaxon but also my own instincts; moving as one with my pack but also deeply alone. Fueled by the moon I pushed myself to run faster, hurdling over fallen logs and skidding around tight corners. Once I was deep in the woods, my legs moved on their own and my mind became clear—crystal clear, with images of my fated mate. Small sparks of worry came and went. I'd never been with a human omega before, and even my wolf was finding it confusing about how we'd overcome the challenge of telling him about who I really was...

But among all the moments of worry were huge waves of excitement. I'd found my fated mate! The joy of it kept me running hard and fast, my heart pounding even faster every time I thought about what our kids might look like once we'd mated.

By the time I tumbled out of the woods and back to the Lodge, my concerns were blurred by the excitement of what could be between us. As I walked across the grounds, I shifted back and immediately shivered as the cold night air hit my face. I rushed to get inside the Lodge where I found most of the pack eating, laughing and chatting.

"Linc!" Jaxon called. I spun around, looking for him, and then felt a hand on my shoulder.

"Hey!" I smiled and brought him into a tight hug. I was still buzzing from the run and could feel the pride radiating off him after leading his pack under the moon. "And congratulations again."

"Hey, congratulations to you," he said, patting me on the back.

My breath caught, and I had to clear my throat before I pulled back from the hug. "For what?" I asked, trying to play it cool.

Jaxon raised his eyebrows and gave me a knowing look, like I didn't need to play dumb.

"How did you know? Did Nicole tell you?"

He laughed and shook his head. "Good guess, but no. I felt it when you did."

When I frowned in confusion he went on to explain. "At the hospital, when you first locked eyes with him. The energy between fated mates is particularly intense. All of our wolves were on high alert, do you remember?"

I nodded and bit my bottom lip. There was something comforting about having my pack involved in this, but it was also a bit uncomfortable and embarrassing, especially if I fucked it all up.

I let out a deep sigh. "I guess that confirms it really is fated, huh?"

Jaxon nodded and put a hand on my shoulder again, giving it a tight squeeze. "It's wonderful news. But I understand more than anyone the hesitation you're feeling."

"Just my luck to land a human omega, huh? Why am I always copying you?" I laughed, and Jaxon grinned.

"You saw him tonight though. How did it go?" Jaxon asked, looking at me with serious eyes. "Is it already getting serious?"

I swallowed dryly and frowned. "I'm not sure... But I want it to be. I'm not sure how he feels, or how fast to move."

Jaxon nodded and was about to say something when Gavin appeared beside us.

"What's all this serious talk about?" he asked.

"This man's fated mate," Jaxon said with a proud smile. Gavin raised his eyebrows and grinned at me.

"Well that is serious! Congratulations!"

"How am I going to…" I shook my head and sighed.

"How are you going to what?" Gavin asked, glancing between us with a confused look on his face.

"The fated mate is a human omega," Nicole interjected as she came up behind Gavin, explaining the problem to him.

"Oooh," Gavin said as he stepped back and welcomed her into the circle. "That's tricky."

"It doesn't have to be," Jaxon said firmly. "There are plenty of shifters who've had human mates, myself included."

"Sure, but you claimed Bryce, made him one of us. What if Shawn doesn't want to become a shifter?" I asked.

"That's something to deal with if it happens. You're getting ahead of yourself," Jaxon said, pulling me into line. "There's no point worrying about that now. The most important thing is to tell him who you are as soon as possible."

The words hit me like a baseball bat to the head. "As soon as possible?"

Jaxon nodded firmly. His face was set in a serious expression and I couldn't help but feel intimidated as hell. He was putting out some serious alpha energy.

"Here's the reality, Linc," he said gruffly. "Shawn might not want to be in a relationship with a shifter."

I swallowed dryly. "So I shouldn't ruin it by telling him…"

"No. You should tell him. He's going to find out eventually. If you aren't honest with him upfront, withholding that kind of information could ruin any chances of a relationship. I learned that the hard way. You have to give him the choice as early as possible. It's the only hope you have for things to work out between you."

I felt my stomach drop and my wolf lie down in my chest with a heavy sigh. All of the daydreaming about our future cubs seemed ridiculous now. Like Jaxon had said, I'd been getting ahead of myself.

"I'm telling you as your alpha," he said, squeezing my shoulder once more. "Tell him as soon as you can."

***

The week dragged on as Christmas and my date with Shawn approached. Everyone in Timberwood Cove went above and beyond with the Christmas cheer. The town was lit up with lights, covered in decorations, and packed full of carolers for the entire week. As per usual I found myself humming Jingle Bells for days. Unfortunately, the fanfare also meant a lot of people took off on vacations, and my regular in-town clients were either away or hosting families at their homes, which meant they didn't want any carpentry or handyman work done until the new year.

Jaxon kept me busy on the shifter homestead with small projects, but not quite busy enough. I found myself left with long hours between jobs and nothing to do to distract myself from the grumbling in my chest every time I thought about my upcoming date with Shawn.

On Tuesday, Christmas Eve, I found myself thinking about him when I was halfway down a ladder, having just cleaned out the gutters of the roof of Gavin's house. All of a sudden, I thought about the way his lips had felt when he'd first kissed me, and my legs almost gave out under me. I gripped the sides of the ladder with my gloved hands and let out a breath through pursed lips. My knees were still shaking when I got to the ground.

Wednesday was Christmas Day, and I had a small breakfast with Cole and gave him a couple of presents before I dropped him off at Nicole's for their yearly special long weekend together. He'd been ecstatic about the new bike he got, and had called Liam on our way over to Nicole's.

"It's *bright blue!*" he yelled.

"Mine too!" I heard Liam shout through the phone.

"What? They match? So cool!" Cole replied.

I was happy to leave him at his mother's, but I worried being alone would drive me crazy. I was kept busy by fixing up the fence palings outside the apartment building where the elders of the Timberwood Cove Pack lived. I was kneeling down with hammer in hand, poising to pound a nail into a fence paling, when I remembered the moment my eyes had locked onto Shawn's at the hospital. My hand slipped and I barely pulled my thumb away in time before the hammer smashed down on the wood right where I'd been gripping the nail.

"Shit!"

I fell back onto my ass and sat in the cold, wet earth. I felt my butt getting numb from the frozen ground as I tried to breathe through the emotions rattling around in my chest. I felt my wolf whimpering and pawing, begging me to go and seek out Shawn now. My heartbeat accelerated to a point where I had to close my eyes and try to get myself, and my wolf, to calm down, which I did by taking deep, slow breaths. No one ever told me that having a fated mate would feel so all-encompassing, so intense.

By Friday, I'd weathered so many of those small hiccups I was confident I'd mastered the art of keeping my wolf composed. Little did I know how crazy I'd feel as I waited at Kay's Diner for Shawn to arrive for dinner.

I sat in a booth at the back where I had a direct view of the door, and not a single bell rang without my eyes shooting up from the menu to check if it was Shawn who had just walked in. Every time it wasn't him, I clenched my jaw and told myself to relax. I put a hand on my knee to stop it from bouncing, and took long, deep, calming breaths while I focused on which oversized burger I was going to order.

But when Shawn arrived, I didn't need to look up. I knew it was him. My wolf started going crazy before he even got to the door. It was sprinting back and forth inside my chest, wanting me to jump out of my seat, grab Shawn and *claim* him. I clenched my jaw and stared down at the menu. The lines were blurred but I didn't dare look up. What if I couldn't control myself? I heard the bell ring and felt a gust of cold air blow into the diner.

"Hey there, Shawn," I heard the waiter say.

"Hi, Cameron."

"Want your usual?"

"No, not tonight. I'm just meeting someone…" I heard Shawn pause, and that was when I looked up.

Our eyes locked. Time slowed down again. He was even more handsome than I'd remembered. His blond hair was slicked back and he wore a white patterned shirt and a navy-blue sweater under a long black overcoat. His pants had a smart seam down the front and I felt a twinge of worry as I realized that I might be underdressed in my "best" flannel shirt, bomber jacket and jeans. He didn't seem to notice though. His eyes were fixed on me, and a huge smile spread across his face as he came over. I barely contained myself as I stood up, doing my best to move unhurriedly.

"Hey, Shawn," I said, hoping my voice didn't come out creaky.

"Hey, you." His voice was sweet and friendly. He walked over and brought me into a warm, welcoming hug. I practically melted before he let go and slid into the booth. I sat opposite him and wondered how he seemed so cool and collected, but then I remembered exactly why—he was a human. This wasn't instinctual for him. It was just a casual date as far as he was concerned. He didn't have a wolf inside him, practically howling for us to become mates.

"It's nice to see you," he said, a hint of amusement lacing his tone, as if he *did* know there was something inside that wanted him.

"I'm really happy to see you." I leaned over and placed my hand on his. It was the most restrained thing I could manage to do.

"Have you eaten here before?" he asked, pulling his hand away and looking down at the menu.

"Uh, a few times." It was a lie—Cole had dragged me there more times than I cared to admit.

"The veggie burger is surprisingly tasty." He pointed it out to me on the menu. His fingers were so close to me, I could almost feel them. I loved how confident he was. It spoke to the alpha in me. I didn't like wimpy, submissive omegas. I looked up and found his gaze again.

"Then that's what I'll get."

We ordered our burgers and a couple of beers, and then made some small talk. I kept one hand on my knee to stop it from shaking. When our food arrived, I watched as Shawn licked his lips at the sight of his burger, and I clenched my jaw as I imagined him licking his lips at the sight of me...

"How long have you lived at the Country Club?" he asked after he swallowed his first bite.

"Since I was born." I didn't see any harm in telling Shawn a few things about me. If he was to become my mate, if I was to claim him, then he'd need to know all of it anyway, and Jaxon had told me to tell Shawn sooner rather than later. But I still wanted to be careful not to frighten him away, and the last thing I wanted to do was break the truth about shifters in the middle of Kay's Diner.

"Huh..." Shawn frowned and cocked his head to the side. "I'm surprised I haven't met you or seen you around town before."

"Well, I don't go into hospitals much, but I'm always around town. I just guess we've simply missed each other. I help out Jaxon with the little league baseball teams, so if you were a fan of baseball you would have seen me there."

"Jaxon? Jaxon Parsons? The pitcher who played for the Takoma Timberwolves? Oh, that's where I knew him from. I thought I recognized him in the delivery ward."

With the conversation taken off me for a while, I wanted to know more about Shawn. "How long have you been here?"

"Oh, quite a few years. I, um, left home when, um, a relationship fell through."

I could see he was feeling awkward about that particular topic, so I asked another question. "Did you have family in town for the holidays?"

"No, they're all back in Vermont. I do usually go back for Christmas, but work has been so busy this year. Plus, I don't think LuLu wanted to go." He smiled and began to relax again. "Did you and Cole have a nice Christmas?"

"We did. Cole got the bike he wanted, but not the telescope that can take photos." I grinned, remembering Cole's small moan about that, but as an eight-year-old he couldn't get *everything* he wanted. "Hey, do you want to go for a walk after this?"

"Yes," he said softly. I caught his eye and a sweet smile spread across his face. "I would like that. Very much."

After dinner, we wandered across the road from Kay's Diner and down to the foreshore. As we stepped down to the beach, a cold wind blew off the ocean. Shawn pulled gloves out from the inside of his coat, and I grabbed mine from the back pocket of my jeans. My wolf felt calmer now, just from being around Shawn, but it was still whimpering for me to get closer to him.

"Do I need to get you home at any particular time?" I asked as I reached out and took his hand. My breath caught for a moment as his gloved fingers stiffened, but then he slowly squeezed my hand. I let out a long, relaxing exhale and melted into the feeling of his hand in mine.

"No, I have tomorrow off, so I'm all yours tonight." His voice caught at the end. I glanced over at him and found his eyes looking out at the dark water. I followed his gaze as we walked down the beach. The sound of the waves lapping softly against the sand calmed me down a little, but I still had to have a conversation with him about shifters, and to be truthful, it wasn't something I was looking forward to.

We walked in silence under the star spotted sky, and a warm thrill moved through me every time Shawn's fingers squeezed mine. We stopped for a moment and looked out at the water. He pulled his hand from mine, but then wrapped his arm around my waist. I only realized how tense I'd been when I felt the stress dissolve from my muscles under his touch. I let out a sigh and draped an arm across his shoulders, gently pulling him to me so he could lean on me.

When Shawn shifted a little bit, I looked down at him.

"Can I walk you home?" I asked.

"Please," he said, his voice sounding smooth and confident.

We wandered down the rest of the beach, hand in hand, and then turned into town when we reached the aquarium. With my hand in his, everything in Timberwood Cove seemed more romantic. Nearly every building sparkled with Christmas lights, while patches of ice on the sidewalk shimmered like diamonds. I stole glances at the side of Shawn's face and often caught him looking at me. It was so hard not to lean into him and steal a kiss too.

When we eventually turned down Pack Lane, my heart started beating even harder. We were almost at Shawn's house and I was almost out of time to start the conversation about shifters. I searched for the right words, but my mind grew more blank with every step we took up the path to his front door.

He cleared his throat as we reached the threshold, while I felt the lump in *my* throat growing bigger. I dragged my eyes up to meet his. I didn't want this to end. I didn't want him to stop looking at me like that, and he might once he found out what I was.

"So," Shawn said.

"So." Maybe I could ask him for another date, tell him then... I was about to ask him when he pressed his lips against mine. They were so warm and soft, and held a small amount of desperation I could relate to. I kissed him back, pulling him against my body, not wanting to let him go.

"Would you like to come inside?" he asked when he drew away. He ran his hand down my chest, and I automatically nodded. Shawn beamed at me, quickly unlocking the door. I saw LuLu's paws before anything else, reaching up to Shawn's legs as she jumped in excitement to see him.

"Hello, hello, my darling," he said as he gently pushed her back.

"Hi LuLu," I said, making my way inside behind them.

"Bed, LuLu!" Shawn closed the door as he gave the order. LuLu glanced excitedly from him to me and then back to him again, then she darted inside to the open living area and jumped into a large dog bed.

"Where were we?" Shawn asked, turning back to me and dragging his gaze over my body. My heart surged as he wet his lips and stepped closer.

"We were..." My wolf scrambled inside me with desire, urging me to pounce, pin him, and take him. I clenched my jaw and took a step back. "Um..."

Shawn frowned and cocked his head to the side. "What's wrong?"

"I don't want to move too fast," I said, stalling.

"We can go slow," Shawn said, reaching down to my hip and tugging me closer to him. "All night..."

I let out a soft moan of desire as my cock swelled in my pants. I wanted nothing more than to drag him into bed and spend the night with him... But orders were orders. Shawn raised his eyebrows and smiled.

"Actually, there's something I need to tell you."

"Tell me?"

Oh god. He was going freak.

I nodded and then glanced over his shoulder at the couch. "Can we sit down?"

"Of course," he said, his voice trembling. He motioned for me to go ahead. LuLu lifted her head as I walked past and I gave her a soft pat before lowering myself onto the couch. Shawn stood in front of me with his arms crossed, chewing his bottom lip and frowning.

"I think you should sit," I said in encouragement, motioning to the seat next to me. He just shook his head and blinked quickly.

"I feel really...confused," he said shortly.

"Please." I reached out and took his hand, tugging it gently. "Sit with me."

"You don't have to break it to me so gently," he murmured as he relented and sat beside me. "I can take a hint."

I let out a sigh and ran a hand through my hair. "This is going to sound ridiculous... But it's really not you... It's me."

Shawn laughed hollowly and shook his head, looking up at the ceiling. He blinked rapidly and I wondered if he was holding back tears.

"Did I come on too strong?" he asked.

"No, of course not. Shawn... I'm really into this," I said, reaching for his hand and squeezing it. He squeezed back but still wouldn't look at me.

"Sorry, I'm being ridiculous," he said, wiping his eyes with his thumb. "It's just been really hard lately. I thought you and I could just have some fun, nothing serious, but here I am crying!"

I put my other hand on his knee. "Well... I want something serious with you."

Shawn sniffed sharply and finally looked right at me. "No, you don't."

I almost laughed. The moment our eyes first met a feeling of complete recognition had moved through me. My wolf had clawed at my chest in a mad frenzy. Shawn was my fated mate. Of course I wanted something serious with him. "I do, but I need to tell you something—"

"No, you don't. Trust me. I'm not someone a good guy like you would settle down with."

"What? Why do you think that?" I frowned, tilting my head.

"I'm just not," he said, inhaling sharply and looking away again. I heard a small huff coming from beside the couch and looked over to find LuLu had lowered her head and let out a sad sigh. When I turned back, Shawn was looking right at me. His jaw was jutted forward in determination and he looked like he was using all of his courage to explain.

He let go of my hand and placed his in his lap before whispering, "I need you to know that I can't have kids."

My heart ached at how much pain flashed over his face as he spoke. I held his gaze as I nodded.

"I'm infertile. If that's a deal-breaker, then let's just keep this casual," he said, sounding like he was already sure it was a deal breaker.

"It's not," I said. I went to reach for his hand, but then I hesitated and put my hand back in my lap. "It's not a deal breaker. I'm interested in you, exactly as you are."

Shawn swallowed and then looked away for a moment before flicking his eyes back to mine.

"We've only had one date, Linc. You don't even know me."

My wolf whined in discomfort and I felt my stomach tightening with anxiety. It was now or never.

"I do know you, Shawn. I...come from a different type of...community. We have a...way to recognize who we're meant to be with," I said. *Wow, that was real clear.* Shawn was frowning and looking at me like I wasn't making any sense. Which was fair. I had no idea how to ease a human into the topic of wolf shifters. I wish I'd asked Jaxon exactly what to say.

"If we're talking about potential deal breakers..." I cleared my throat. "I have a big one."

Shawn moved in his seat to face me more directly, and then crossed his hands in his lap, waiting patiently for me to continue. When I didn't, he asked, "Worse than being infertile?"

I gave a short laugh and nodded. "Much more extreme."

"Well, honey, don't keep me hanging!" He swatted my chest, and I laughed again. I could barely believe what I was about to say.

"I know you've heard the rumors about wolves in Timberwood Cove. Well, wolves have great instincts. Instincts about everything—food, direction, other predators, people. Mates..."

Shawn nodded, but I could see in his eyes he was deeply confused about where I was going with this. My heart was practically knocking against my ribcage as I thought about Shawn's reaction. He could be okay with it. He could think I was crazy. He could simply not want to be with me *because* I was a shifter. He could...do all manner of things, but there was only one way to find out. I sucked in a deep breath. "And you're my mate."

"Your mate? Uh... Are you like...a furry?"

"No! I'm, uh... Well..." I searched Shawn for any sign that this was a bad idea, that he'd immediately blab my secret to the rest of Timberwood Cove and expose my whole pack, but my instincts told me I could trust him. My wolf nudged me. "I'm a wolf shifter."

Shawn stared at me.

I bit my lip and waited. He squinted his eyes. I swallowed dryly.

"Is this a joke?"

"No. I'm serious. I come from a pack that's been in this area for hundreds of years and—
"

"You know what? I think you should leave." Shawn's eyes were wild with anger as he went to stand. I put my hand on his arm to stop him.

"Shawn, please, I'm *serious*," I insisted. "I'm trying to tell you why I *know* we're meant to be together."

"Oh my god, Linc." Shawn let out an exasperated sigh. "You sound crazy. You know that, right?"

"Yes, but I need you to believe me anyway."

"You really expect me to believe that, not only do you know we're *mates*, but you're a wolf?" Shawn's skepticism was better than his anger, but it was obvious he was pessimistic.

"Do you want me to show you?" I asked because I couldn't think of any other way to convince him.

"Oh, please be my guest!" Shawn leaned back against the couch and crossed his arms over his chest. His whole attitude didn't bode well, but I had to try. He was my mate, and I didn't to lose him even though shifting could do exactly that.

I stood, made my way to the center of the room and...shifted.

Chapter 6 - Shawn

My jaw dropped. I *could not believe* there was a wolf standing in my living room. I couldn't believe I'd just watched the man I was seriously crushing over literally transform into a *wolf*. If Trevor hadn't mentioned their existence just a few days before, I would have been *certain* I was truly losing my mind.

Then again, hadn't I accused Trevor of losing touch with reality? And now, here I was face-to-face with the plot of a novel that millions of people bought when they wanted to read some sexy fantasy romances. Surely this was a dream. A very realistic and freaky dream. And judging by the feeling in my pants, it was about to be a wet dream. I had no idea what my subconscious was trying to tell me; probably that I needed to get laid, but I wasn't scared, exactly, just...startled, and exhilarated, and... I pinched my thigh. It stung. Which meant I was awake.

"What... the fuck?"

My heart beat a frantic tattoo. I'd never been this close to a wolf before. I'd never wanted to, either. Wolves are big, they're strong, they have sharp teeth, and they only have allegiance to their own kind. Or so I thought.

This wolf, the one in my house—Linc—was, admittedly, majestic. I stared at him unapologetically. He had long legs the color of cream, with caramel colored fur from his belly to his shoulders. The caramel fur was mottled with black from the top of his head down to his tail, which was as bushy as a fox tail and had a fully black tip. His nose was black and wet. His eyes were a rich toffee swirl; and fixed on me. His gaze was head-on, confident, warm, and intelligent. The same as Linc's human eyes, I realized. Suddenly his super-alpha behavior made a lot more sense. He was a *literal* wolf! That's why the way he pursued me was so intense and laser-focused. It was his canine instincts that kept him hot on my trail.

I wasn't sure what to do. I didn't know if he could talk while he was in his wolf form, so we just gazed at each other in silence. I took a deep breath and tried to accept what my eyes were seeing. I was actually a little freaked out. My whole body felt frozen, as if getting ready to go into fight or flight mode, but not yet making its mind up which one to do. I tried another deep breath. It didn't do anything for me.

As I sat there, motionless, Linc's human form re-emerged and the wolf disappeared. I was able to take a slightly deeper breath once I saw the handsome face I recognized. But I was still dazed. He took a tentative step toward me. As he got closer my skin heated and my cock began to tingle. I even felt myself getting wet with slick.

This can't be happening. I can't be falling for a shifter. Don't they have litters *of cubs? Surely that would mean Linc would want more than just Cole. He's bound to want more children, and I can't give him any.*

As Linc took another step toward me, I panicked, needing to say something before I gave in to my arousal and complicated things. I leaned back just a little and held my hands out. "Linc, I um, I don't think... That's um..."

"A deal breaker?" Linc asked, his voice trembling so much I was worried he was on the verge of crying.

Hot tears started filling my eyes in empathy, and my nose threatened to run. I sniffed and willed my eyes to stay dry so I could convince him I was all wrong for him. "N-not necessarily," I said, watching with wide eyes as he sat down on the couch beside me. My body *itched* for him to touch me, but my brain insisted I had to end this. "Why would you risk showing me...that? I mean, what if I just freaked out?"

Linc grinned. "You're *not* freaked out?"

"Of course am! Oh my *god*, Linc! But what if I ran out of here screaming and told everyone about you and your pack?"

Linc lowered his head but continued to gaze at me, his human eyes just as beautiful as his wolf ones. "I had to trust you. I had to be honest."

"But why me?" I asked in a tiny voice that came out like a squeak.

"Because you're my mate, Shawn. We're meant to be together."

"You don't know that," I said reflexively.

"I do, it's part of being a wolf shifter. When we find our mate, we *know*. Call it a sixth sense, if you like. But my wolf recognized its mate in you. You belong to us, heart, body and soul."

"No, my body isn't...right for you." I dropped my gaze to my lap, trying to hold back feelings of shame.

"Shawn. I don't care if we can have kids or not. I *know* we both need each other. Can't you feel it?"

I did feel something very intense, and I had ever since we met. I felt drawn to him, connected to him, attracted on a very instinctual level. I had chalked it up to being flattered, horny, and lonely. But now, I searched Linc's eyes like he did mine, looking to see if he could be telling the truth.

"Don't you believe in true love?" Linc asked me.

"Yeah, I think I do." At that admission, the tears teetering precariously on my lower eyelids fell gently down my cheeks. I sniffed and wiped at my face with the sleeve of my shirt.

"Haven't you ever seen a falling star and wished you would meet the person you were meant to be with for the rest of your life?" Linc asked now.

I felt a sob rise in my throat. Tears were pouring now, but I ignored them and concentrated on breathing normally. "This can't be real," I reiterated, my voice wobbling. "It sounds like... A stupid romance novel!" I started laughing as I remembered Trevor again. What would he say if I told him what he thought was a rumor was factual? My laughter turned back to sobbing and I felt like my heart was falling apart like wet paper.

"I know," Linc said gently, moving a little closer to me. "But it *is* real."

He reached out and gently brushed a tear from my cheek with the knuckle of his forefinger. His touch felt more electric than ever before, and my muscles immediately began to relax. I let out a soft, involuntary moan, and felt my dick pressing against the front of my pants. My slick was getting out of control, threatening to soak all the way through my underwear.

"Can't you feel the magic between us?" he asked, so softly, so *earnestly*, I couldn't deny the answer. I was in the middle of a swirling whirlpool of fate; almost being swept away, and yet on a deep level I felt calm and peaceful, like I never had before. All that was left was to fall into my mate's outstretched arms.

As soon as I did, as soon as his lips touched mine, I was suddenly, and fully, in heat. I'd never felt it come on so fast before, nor so overwhelmingly powerful. I doubted either Linc or I could have controlled ourselves, not then. I certainly didn't want to. Being an omega in heat wasn't always particularly easy when around an alpha. Not that we were pushed into doing something we didn't want to but being in heat definitely made omegas more horny; well it did with me.

Linc groaned and dragged me closer to his hard body. I went willingly, wrapping my arms around his neck, allowing him to press his tongue into my mouth, actually begging him to with my moans.

In heat, I wanted him, *needed* him, and I'm sure he knew that. He picked me up as if I weighed nothing and carried me to my bedroom.

"I'm in heat," I managed to say in between ferocious kisses, as if he couldn't tell by the unique musk I was giving off.

"I know. Don't worry, I'm going to take care of you." He gently placed me on the bed and started tugging at my pants and underwear. I whimpered as my ass pulsed and slick began to coat the inside of my thighs. Linc grinned, but then he cupped the side of my face. "But just to let you know, I've never done this with a guy before."

"You've never..."

Linc shook his head. "I've only ever been with Nicole. After we broke up I focused on Cole. I've never had time or the energy for anyone else, but now I've met you..."

"You sure?"

"Oh yes. I'm very sure. I want you, Shawn, so much." He leaned down and kissed me again, this time tenderly but with a thoroughness that seemed even more intense than his passionate ones. When he pulled back, he was grinning again.

I scrambled to pull my shirt off while trying to get Linc's off too. He laughed, stripping for me until we were both panting and naked. Then he crawled over the top of me and stared into my eyes. I wasn't sure what he was waiting for, if he wanted me to say something, but he merely smiled.

"My mate," he said softly, and then he pushed one of my legs up and slipped two fingers easily inside my wet hole. And then, whether it was instinct or not, he stroked them across my prostate.

"Oh my *god*!" I clapped a hand over my mouth lest I scream bloody murder and make my neighbors call the cops. My entire body lit up as he pushed his fingers deeper. I arched my back and grabbed the base of my cock, willing myself not to come yet. Linc was focused on my ass, biting his lower lip as he watched the way his fingers moved in and out my hole. I shuddered, barely thinking clearly, an orgasm already sliding down my spine and lodging in my balls. My slick poured over his hand, making his way easier, and he took advantage, slipping in a third finger.

"Oh my *god*, Linc. Oh my god." I gasped and writhed beneath him, so ready for him to fill me. My heat was making my hole ache for his cock so badly, I would have done *anything* to be fucked by him. I bucked my hips, trying to get his fingers deeper inside me.

"You feel *fucking* amazing," Linc said breathlessly. "Are you ready for me?"

"Yes. Oh, yes! Take me now."

He carefully pulled his fingers out of my ass and held them up to his face, inhaling deeply. "Mm. You smell better than anything I've ever smelled in my *life*."

Fuck that was sexy. Linc *was sexy.*

"Linc, please. *Now*. Right now." I tried to push my ass closer to him, beyond desperate, feeling pitifully empty now his fingers weren't inside me.

Linc's hard cock pointed toward me, the tip dripping with precum. I moaned, my body flushing as I imagined his immense girth filling me. There was a shine in his eyes as he put a hand on the bed next to my head. He leaned down to kiss me and I parted my lips, willing him to take my mouth as deeply as he took my ass. And then, blessedly, I felt the head of his cock press against me. I moaned as he slowly, incredibly pushed himself into me. He kept pressing, inch after inch, and I moaned louder into his mouth every time. The more of his cock I took, the better I felt.

"Fuck, you're so tight," Linc groaned against my lips when he was more than halfway in.

"Don't stop." *Oh please, he'd better not stop.*

"No. I'm going to take you so deep you'll be sitting awkwardly for the next month."

I think I would have laughed if he hadn't started flexing his hips once more and eased another few inches of his cock into my ass. Once he was fully seated, I grabbed my knees to pull my legs up as far as I could get them, and he started thrusting. Gently at first, and then faster, harder, until we were one writhing, gyrating mess of hormones and animalistic sounds. His breath was hot against my neck, and his deep grunts echoed in my ear.

As he continued to fuck me I wrapped my arms around his neck, quivering with each thrust of his cock against my prostate. It was as if he was aiming for that exact spot, and every time he hit it I felt myself edging closer and closer to a powerful climax. My eyes rolled back in my head, and just as I reached for that sweet release, Linc's cock seemed to swell somehow, filling me even more.

"Oh my god! What the..." My hole stretched to accommodate him, but the base of his cock was so thick he could barely move. He arched his neck and howled, managing to thrust another half an inch before a wave of hot pleasure rocked through me, so intense I could hardly breath. I spasmed, gasping, clinging to him as rope after rope of creamy cum sprayed Linc's broad chest.

He groaned as my ass clenched around him, and then he thrust into me one more time, holding himself still as he shot what felt like a fountain of seed deep inside me.

Afterward, we lay in a tangled heap of heavy limbs, lost in complete oblivion for what felt like hours.

Chapter 7 - Linc

Morning light filtered in through the sides of Shawn's blackout curtains and I slowly woke. My toes tingled. In fact, they felt kind of wet. I moaned and rolled over, wrapping an arm around Shawn, and sank into the pleasure of how warm and heavy he felt, deep in sleep. I wriggled my toes back under the covers and tried to doze back off, indulging in the feeling of being beside my mate and still blissed out from last night. I'd never felt anything like it. It wasn't just because he was the first male omega I'd ever been with, but because he was my *mate*. His being in heat of course was an added bonus, and I smiled as I remembered the way he'd begged me, frantic to have me inside him. I know he didn't feel the same way I did about our fated connection, but to hear the soft whimpers he made, to experience that look on his face as he came... And I'd knotted him...

I was on the brink of dozing off but was quickly woken again by the feeling of a cold, wet nose pressed against my foot and a soft, warm tongue licking at my big toe. I groaned and sat up, and then pulled the blanket back. LuLu's fuzzy face looked up at me with sad, pathetic puppy-dog eyes. She glanced from me to the door and back again.

"Is it time for your walk?" I asked quietly, glancing at the clock. It was past nine, and Shawn showed no signs of stirring. I planted a soft kiss on his cheek and nuzzled his neck, whispering sweet words to bring him out of his sleep. All I got in response was a grunt, and he rolled away from me, pulling the blankets up over his face.

"Your dad's not a morning person, huh?" I asked LuLu. She sighed and rested her chin on her paws, then looked pleadingly toward the door.

"Alright, c'mon then," I relented. "We'll go for a walk."

The corgi immediately jumped off the bed and trotted out of the bedroom. I yawned and pulled myself out of bed before grabbing my clothes and throwing them on as I followed her. I stopped in the bedroom doorway to look back at Shawn. My wolf sighed contentedly, and I felt my heart flutter. I had to take last night's reaction to my wolf as encouraging—despite his initial hesitations, he'd been okay when I'd shifted back into my human form. There was no way that wasn't a positive sign... Right?

It was easy to find LuLu's leash, hung up beside the front door. Everything in Shawn's house was exactly where I expected it to be. The whole place was neat and tidy. As I clipped LuLu's leash onto her collar, I wondered if he hired a cleaning service, or if he had the time to keep things so clean himself. Either way, I liked it. It was a nice change from the rustic chaos that my hand-built woodsy home was filled with.

I zipped up my jacket and braced myself for the cold air as I opened the front door. LuLu trotted down the front steps ahead of me. I squinted up at the sky and smiled when a small ray of sunshine broke through the heavy clouds. LuLu glanced back at me and seemed to glare, then waited patiently for me to catch up. I hurried up and followed her as she led the way to the dog park.

I'd left my gloves at Shawn's so as soon as I unclipped LuLu's leash, I shoved my hands in my pockets to warm them up. That's when my phone buzzed. It was Jaxon.

"Hi," I answered.

"So, it went well," he said rather than asked.

I let out a laugh as I looked up at the sky. The ray of sunshine had disappeared and the whole sky had returned to its usual December gray, but everything still seemed brighter and more beautiful to me.

"Yes, it went well."

"You told him," he said.

"Actually, I showed him. He was a little shocked at first, but he's fine with it."

"Well, that's great, I'm so happy for you."

I laughed again and looked out across the park as LuLu came trotting back over to me. "Thanks, Jax. I'm happy, too."

"Hey, Cole's trying to get my attention, hang on." Jax pulled the phone away from his mouth and I heard my son's muted voice in the background.

"He's asking how your night was," Jax said with a chuckle.

"Tell him it was fun."

"It was fun," Jaxon said to Cole. As I knelt down and reattached LuLu's collar, Jax continued to talk to Cole.

"Ask him yourself," Jax finally said, and I heard him put me on speakerphone.

Cole immediately came through loud and clear. "If he's friends, can we go to the beach to watch stars with him?"

"Sure, I'll ask Shawn if he wants to."

"Tonight?"

"I'll ask. Are you having a good sleepover with Liam?"

"Yeah, and baby Lori is awesome. I wish I had a—"

"Okay, I gotta go," I said before Cole could say any more. "Jax, I'll come by around noon?"

"Perfect."

I slid my phone into my back pocket then massaged my face. I was smiling so hard it hurt. LuLu and I headed up Pack Street to grab two coffees from a cafe. The barista raised her eyebrows at me when I asked if she knew Shawn's order.

"The nurse who lives just down there," I said, pointing toward his house. "With the corgi?" I pointed to LuLu.

"Oh I know who you mean. I'm just impressed someone is ordering a coffee for him for once. It's about time. He's a super nice guy." She put his cappuccino and my latte in a cardboard tray and slid a baby-sized paper cup into it beside ours. "Puppuccino for LuLu," she explained with a wink. "It's her usual order. Can't start her day without one."

I thanked her, and then headed back to Shawn's house. LuLu seemed happy that I was carrying her treat and walked right beside me. Everyone respects an alpha who provides what they need.

But as we turned into Shawn's yard her ears pricked up and she started whimpering. It took me a moment, but I heard it too.

"LuLu?" Shawn cried from inside his house. "Where are you?" He sounded frantic, and I bounded up the steps.

"She's here!" I said as I opened the door. Shawn turned to me, his eyes wide. I dropped LuLu's leash so she could run to him. He gasped and bent down to welcome her into his arms before picking her up and cradling her like a baby as she happily licked his face.

"Oh god, I thought you were gone." He squeezed her, almost sobbing. He glanced up, and an embarrassed expression washed over his face as he saw what I was carrying.

"You went for coffee," he said, wiping his eyes.

"You seemed like you could use a little caffeine when I tried to wake you up," I said softly as I closed the door behind me. Shawn sighed and sat down on the couch. He unclipped LuLu's leash and she rushed back over to me, jumping up and trying to get to the coffees as I put them on the kitchen counter. I gave a quiet growl and she immediately sat down.

"I thought you'd...gone," Shawn said with a little hiccup.

"Gone? No, baby, I'm not going anywhere." The fact that Shawn thought I'd leave him put daggers in my heart. I wanted him to trust that I'd never leave him, but I knew it would take time to build that trust.

He put his head in his hands and mumbled something into them. I brought his cappuccino over to him, and he looked up as he took it from me.

"I'm sorry. I didn't mean to think that, but the last time I went to bed with someone and woke up alone..." He shuddered, as if cold. "My ex decided I wasn't good enough for him because I couldn't give him kids. We'd been arguing about it, but I hadn't expected him to just walk out. He never said he was leaving, but I woke up one morning and he was...gone."

There was a tremor in his voice I understood. I sat beside him and stared at the tears still swimming in his beautiful hazel eyes. "Please don't cry, okay. I promise, I'm nothing like your ex," I said gently.

"Do you..." Shawn gazed at me with the same puppy-dog eyes LuLu had given me. "Do you still want to be my mate?"

I knew Shawn may still not get the whole "fated mate" thing, despite my explanations, but that was okay. He'd understand soon enough. "Of course I do. We're fated." I reached over and stroked his jaw with my fingertips. Shawn sighed and rested his cheek against my hand.

"That still sounds so weird," he said. "But I can get used to it."

"I hope so because it means I'm not going anywhere. And I definitely wouldn't steal your dog."

Shawn gave me a wobbly smile, and I smiled back, happy he believed me.

I got up to grab my coffee off the bench. "How does LuLu have her, uh, puppuccino?" I asked, pulling the plastic top off the small cup.

"Just put it in her bowl there," Shawn motioned to the dog bowl beside the sink. I poured the frothed milk out into the bowl and watched, perplexed, as LuLu lapped it up. "Don't worry, it's good for her. They use non-dairy milk and add some vitamins for dogs or something."

"Maybe I should order that next time," I said. Shawn let out a laugh and nearly on his cappuccino.

"Too soon for jokes?" I asked, sitting beside him on the couch.

"Everything is going so fast," Shawn said, putting a hand on my knee. "The jokes are just doing their best to keep up."

"Are you keeping up? Or is it too fast? Am I going too fast?" I asked, suddenly worried about everything that had happened the night before. Shawn quickly quelled my fears by smiling and shaking his head.

"I'm right here with you," he said.

My wolf let out a happy sigh, and I leaned in to press my lips against Shawn's. A warm glow started in the middle of my chest and flowed outward. I moaned as his tongue slipped into my mouth. I tasted coffee and a slight hint of something new. Something was different from the night before, but I couldn't quite place it…

Shawn gently pulled away and then ran his fingers through my hair. "I'm off work today. Would you like to spend the day with me or do you have to be somewhere?" Shawn asked softly, a small tremor still in his voice.

"I'd love to spend every minute with you. Tonight, Cole wants to know if you'd like to come stargazing with us at the beach?" I asked, then took a sip of my latte.

"Oh, I'd really like that."

"Good, and before that, can I take you to see the homestead?"

Shawn's eyes opened wide. "The gated Country Club? I've always wanted to see what goes on in there," he admitted, suddenly sounding excited.

"It's beautiful, but in reality it's just like the rest of town," I said, not wanting his expectations to be too high. "There's just, uh. One thing…"

"If you need me to swear an oath that I won't tell anyone what I see, or anything about wolves… Then you've got it," he said, holding up his fingers in a Scout's salute.

I laughed. "No it's just… You're no longer in heat, are you? Did you take a suppressor?"

"Oh, um, no. My heat has stopped, I think. I mean, I no longer feel any of the symptoms." He frowned, but then glanced at me through long blond lashes. "That can happen though, you know, when an alpha… And we, um, didn't use condoms. Sorry about that. I should have asked you, but with me not able to get pregnant…"

"That's okay, Shawn. I trust you don't have anything we need to see a doctor for?"

"Oh, no, I don't have anything. And you?"

"Nope, clear." It wasn't always easy to have these conversations, but I was glad Shawn didn't feel too awkward about it. I hadn't been with anyone in years, not since Nicole, which sounded a little pathetic, but I just hadn't met anyone I wanted to be with, not until Shawn.

Shawn smiled, but then cocked his head to the side. "Why did you ask?"

"Well, though the alpha members of my pack will *always* behave themselves, I didn't want you to feel uncomfortable around any of them if you were still in heat."

"Uh, how many of you are there?" he asked nervously.

"Me? Just one. I'm one of a kind."

Shawn shook his head and rolled his eyes.

"You mean how many shifters?" I asked.

He nodded before taking a sip of his drink.

"Well, there are quite a few, but not all of them belong to the Timberwood Cove Pack."

"There's more than one pack in Timberwood Cove?"

"There are a several actually, but my pack is the largest, and we've been here for generations."

"Wow, I had no idea. Well, Trevor seemed to, but I don't think he knew for certain. Do I know any other shifters?" he asked eagerly.

"No doubt you do, we fit in pretty well. Could be your local carpenter, or even your favorite baseball player," I said with a wink.

Shawn frowned and I could practically see the wheels turning in his head.

"Jaxon?" he asked.

I laughed and nodded, then gave Shawn a quick run-down on the shifter dynamic. The only thing I didn't mention was the claiming bite, I felt it might be too much to pile everything on him in one go, but I couldn't help but feel excited at the prospect of officially making him mine and consequently turning him.

"Ready to see it?" I asked before taking a last gulp of my coffee.

"Is it okay if LuLu tags along? She only has doggy daycare during the week."

I grinned, delighted Shawn was ready to see where I lived. "All canines are welcome."

***

My car was still parked up at Kay's Diner so we walked LuLu through the dog park again and up along the sports park. Shawn linked his arm through mine, and as we rounded the corner to walk up Silvercoat Way, he whispered, "Last night was the best sex of my life."

I couldn't describe the thrill that washed over me, but I don't think I'd ever grinned so much. "Me too," I replied, and we shared a huge, happy smile.

From Kay's Diner, I drove us the few blocks to Pack Lane and then headed north, straight up to the Wolf Lodge. Shawn gasped and slapped my arm excitedly as the gates opened. I headed east and drove him the long way around the neighborhood, pointing out houses and parts of the woods that were important to me. His mouth was open and his jaw was practically on the ground. LuLu also seemed excited, and she pressed her nose against the window in the backseat.

"It's so beautiful," Shawn said. "The architecture is exquisite. So detailed. And the landscaping!"

"And what about that fence that a certain someone built?" I nudged him and pointed to the fence I'd put up near the elder's apartments.

He laughed and nodded. "All the fences are beautiful, too."

When I pulled in to Jaxon's driveway I noticed Gavin's car was parked there too. As we approached, I saw Jaxon and Gavin slinking out of the front door and tip-toeing across the porch.

"Bryce and the baby are finally asleep," Jaxon explained quietly as we met them in the yard.

"Lori's been keeping you up at night?" Shawn asked, and I beamed at him, proud he'd remembered the baby's name. LuLu sat patiently at Shawn's feet, glancing around at her surroundings.

"Oh yep, Lori sure is a howler," Jaxon said with a laugh. He then extended a hand to Shawn. "Nice to see you, man."

"You too," Shawn shook Jaxon's hand firmly.

"This is Shawn, he was our nurse." Jaxon introduced Shawn to Gavin. "And now he's uh…"

Jaxon winked at me and I raised my eyebrows. "Here to see the homestead," I said, finishing his sentence for him while placing a supportive hand on Shawn's shoulders. He looked at me and gave me an appreciative smile. "And this is LuLu."

"Nice to meet you both," Gavin said, shaking Shawn's hand and then bending down to rub LuLu's head.

"Gavin is Cole's uncle," I said to give Shawn some context.

"Oh yeah, the boys are around back," Jaxon said and motioned for us to follow him.

As Jax led the way, I reached out and took Shawn's hand. He shot me a shy smile and squeezed my hand. His long fingers were cold so I tugged the sleeve of my jacket down to cover our hands, then looked up as I heard him gasp. LuLu's ears pricked up and we both looked at Shawn to find his eyes were locked on the woods that grew right into Jaxon's backyard.

"Wow. It's so beautiful!" he said as we stepped into the yard.

"Yep, we sure like it here." Gavin smiled as he shut the gate behind us.

"I had no idea there was anywhere this nice in Timberwood Cove," Shawn exclaimed.

Jaxon laughed and slapped Shawn on the back before turning toward the woods and letting out a high-pitched whistle. In less than a second, two rambunctious young wolves spilled out through the brush and tumbled across the yard toward us. Shawn tensed beside me, and LuLu stood to attention. I squeezed his hand. I heard him take a deep breath and felt him start to relax, but LuLu backed up and hid behind his legs.

Cole and Liam shifted back into their human forms but kept running full-speed at us, scarves and coats blowing back behind them as they sprinted. Cole threw himself against me and wrapped his arms around me, almost tackling me to the ground with his momentum. I let go of Shawn's hand to catch Cole.

"Miss me, kiddo?" I asked as I laughed and wrapped my son into a big hug.

"No way," Cole scrunched up his nose and then gave me a beaming smile. "Okay, maybe a little bit."

"Good sleepover?" I asked.

"Liam and I just found a gross dead thing in the woods," he said, pointing to the woods.

"It was disgusting," Liam said, but the huge smiles on both their faces said they'd loved every second of it.

"I hope you left it well alone," Jaxon said, draping an arm over Liam's shoulder.

"Yeah, but it was so rotten, you should have smelled it!" Cole pinched his nose, and then bent down to say hello to LuLu who was shyly peering at him from behind Shawn's leg.

"Boys, this is probably not something Shawn wants to hear about first thing in the morning," Gavin warned.

"Oh, it's fine," Shawn said, waving off his concern. "I'm a nurse, I can stomach anything." We laughed and Shawn smiled, but then let out another sigh as he looked up at the back of Jaxon's house. "I know I keep saying this, but everywhere in the homestead is just so beautiful."

"It's beautiful land up here, and we pride ourselves on our architecture and workmanship," Jaxon said. "We use techniques that have been passed down through our pack for centuries. I'm sure Linc can tell you more about that... It's a shame we can't share more of our land and our culture, but for our safety, people have to be a member of the pack to live here."

"Well, sign me up," Shawn responded.

I glanced at Jaxon and found he was already regarding me. We shared a look, and I knew then I'd been given permission to do exactly that.

Chapter 8 - Shawn

After meeting some more pack members at Jaxon's house, Linc took Cole, LuLu, and me back to his place for lunch. The Country Club was stunning. All the houses seemed to have intricate woodwork and lush gardens. LuLu was right at home, playing with the kids and bounding around in the thick grass. Linc's house was no exception, a sizeable timber home that was so cozy inside, it felt like something from a cabin inspiration magazine.

While Linc rummaged around in the fridge for burger ingredients, Cole grabbed my hand and pulled me upstairs to his room to show me his telescope.

"Here's the finder, here's the focuser, here's the eyepiece. You can't really tell how they all work right now because the sun's out," Cole explained confidently.

"Looks like a sweet unit." I said, impressed that a kid at his age was into space to that extent.

"Yeah, it's pretty good. Sometimes I draw the craters that I find on the moon. Wanna see?" he asked excitedly.

"Definitely." I sat down on his bed and admired the workmanship of the bed frame. The headboard was decorated with wolves and intricate patterns that looked kind of tribal. I wondered if Linc had made it.

Cole pulled a sketchbook out of his desk and flipped it open in my lap.

"Wow, these are really detailed, Cole." I could tell he was proud of them, but I was being honest with my assessment. "Did you use a mechanical pencil?"

"Yeah, I always use a fine point for more accurate drawings," he said proudly.

"Guys!" Linc yelled up the stairs. "It's grill time!"

"*Coming Dad*!" Cole shouted in reply, hurting my eardrum. He turned to me. "My dad makes the *best* burgers."

"I can't wait to try them," I said as we went downstairs.

"Well, I hope you like yours charred. That's the only way he makes them."

"Fine by me, as long as the onions are burnt too. I love burnt onions."

"Me too! But you know what's the best? Onion *rings*."

"That's true. Does your dad make onion rings?"

"No, not yet anyway," Cole replied wistfully. "We can dream…"

***

Cole was right, Linc's burgers were good, although blacker than I usually had mine. We hung out in the backyard, drinking iced tea and playing with LuLu until the sun started to dip low and it became too cold to stay out. When we started packing up supplies for our stargazing field trip, Linc brought out a tent to his car.

"What's…that for?" I asked, a little weary about a sudden camping trip I hadn't agreed on, my mind flicking quickly to bears eating me alive in the woods.

"That's for when Cole gets tuckered out. I thought we could have a mini sleepover on the beach since he tends to get tired early. I'm bringing a few blankets too."

My heart swelled at Linc's attentive style of fatherhood. He was assertive, but not just to get his own way. He also pre-empted the needs of his dependents… Nothing like other alphas I'd known, and *definitely* nothing like Phillip.

Once we got the car packed up we stopped by my place where Cole excitedly wanted to help me get all the parts of my telescope packed into its case. He unfastened and re-fastened the Velcro straps more than a few times and did up each zipper with zeal. He wanted to carry it out to the car too, but not only was it too heavy for him, I didn't want to entrust him with such delicate equipment. It had cost me a pretty penny, so I was firm with my refusal, but he understood, which I thought was mature of him.

At my favorite spot on the beach, we set up the little pop-up tent, spread out blankets on the sand, and got to work setting up the equipment. When everything was done, Linc poured us hot chocolates from a thermos. I held mine close to my chest, smiling at him as he as he looked through my telescope. LuLu ran back and forth on the sand for a while, chasing sea gulls, then toddled her way over to the tent.

"What am I looking at here?" Linc asked.

"Hm, let's see," I said, nudging him out of the way and looking through the viewfinder.

"It just looked kind of black," he said.

"Uh…" I held back a laugh and glanced at him. "You're looking at the lens cap."

He groaned and held his face in his hands in embarrassment. "I told you I needed help with this!" he said before he burst out laughing.

"I didn't know you needed *this* much help!" I chuckled and moved to take off the cap.

"I'm finished, Shawn!" Cole called out, and I turned to find him smiling proudly, sitting beside his telescope.

"Make sure you've got the lens cap off," Linc said.

Cole rolled his eyes and held up the cap. "Duh."

"Let's have a look at what's in the sky!" I said, scooting closer to Cole. Linc followed, sitting close to me and leaning over to be part of the conversation.

"How do we do this?" he asked. "Tell me the basics."

"First, you look at the sky without a telescope. It gives you your bearings, and you see what's up there, and decide what you want to get a closer look at."

"I see the Orion!" Cole said, pointing out the three medium-bright stars in a straight row.

"Good job, Cole," Linc said, praising his son.

"Well spotted," I agreed. "Have you ever seen the nebula above the *club* of Orion?"

Cole shook his head so I helped him to position his telescope, and then sat back to let him look at the nebula. I felt Linc moving closer to me and I leaned into him, enjoying his warmth and his smell.

"Wow," Cole said.

"You're good with kids," Linc whispered. I felt a surge of pride, followed by a sharp stabbing in my heart. I *was* good with kids. I deserved one of my own. Still, the compliment seemed genuine, and I turned to thank him with a small kiss.

"Shawn… Can I look at it through your telescope?" Cole asked in a little voice.

"Of course," I said, and we all scooted over. Linc moved to the other side of Cole and wrapped his arm around his son as I explained how to use the scope and find Orion with the prerecorded settings.

When I'd finished and Cole was off and running with the technology, I realized I hadn't seen LuLu in a while. I went over to the tent to check on her. She had burrowed her way into the blanket that Linc put in there and she was fast asleep. I guessed it had been a big day for all of us. Her head and front paws were sticking out of the blanket, but the rest of her was wrapped up. Her little paws were twitching in the midst of her doggy dream, and I clutched my chest watching her. She just looked so sweet and innocent.

I turned back to the star-spotting set-up and watched Cole showing Linc something through the eyepiece. Linc protectively rested his hand on Cole's back. The wind ruffled their jackets slightly, and as I approached, they both turned to look at me with bright eyes.

"We found Saturn!" Cole exclaimed.

"That's *awesome*," I said. "Will you show me?"

Linc moved out of the way so I could bend down to the eyepiece, and then he moved his hand from Cole's back to mine. My back instantly felt warm and tingly where his hand rested on it. I suddenly remembered the way he'd rested his hand on my face and wiped my tears away this morning. I inwardly smiled, shooting him a quick smile before squinting through the eyepiece.

Cole yawned loudly behind me.

"You tired, bud?" Linc asked him.

"Yeah..."

"LuLu is in the tent if you want to cuddle her," I offered.

Cole nodded, and then scampered off, leaving Linc and me alone.

"Let's get our own blanket," Linc suggested, reaching into the duffel bag he brought from the truck. I helped him lay it across us as the wind whipped it back and forth, then lay down into his inviting arms. The sea air was cold and salty in my lungs, and Linc's shoulder was warm and cozy under my head.

"Thanks for coming out here with us," Linc said, his deep voice sounding breathy and husky near my ear.

"It's my pleasure." Everything I'd done with Linc so far had been wonderful, but also a little unreal. I was amazed how it was both at the same time—extremely unlikely and dramatic, but intimate and natural too. Knowing he felt the same way helped me relax.

"There are so many stars out tonight, even without the telescope, it's so beautiful," I said.

"Makes you think about life in a different way, doesn't it?" he replied, looking up at the sky.

"In what way?"

"How beautiful and amazing the future can be now I've found you." He turned to kiss me, his touch making me want to stay there, curled up in his arms, safe and warm.

"Tell me all about how beautiful this future could be."

"Well, we could move in together when we're ready. Cole already likes you a lot. We can be a family. If we want more kids, we can look into adopting. I just want to grow together and build a perfect life. How about you?"

"That sounds...too good to be true. This is all happening so fast..." It was hard to prevent my emotions from overflowing. I felt elated to be with Linc but also sad thinking about how terribly Phillip treated me, how I had almost given up on love before I met Linc. I took a breath and steadied myself. "I've always wanted that domestic life with a wonderful alpha, kids, and LuLu being pampered like she deserves. Things like cooking together as a family, and pillow fights and—" Just then a falling star flashed across the sky right in front of my eyes. "Did you see that?"

"Yeah!" Linc sat upright. "Wow… Time to make a wish, Shawn."

I closed my eyes and wished for what I really wanted more than anything. The wish was the same, the one I had buried after learning it was impossible, but still yearned for all the same: *I wish to have a child of my own.* Saying it, even silently, reminded me it might be a waste of a wish. *And I wish Linc will never leave me,* I added quickly, just in case.

I opened my eyes to see Linc gazing at me with a small smile. He leaned in and gave me a kiss so tender it made me forget all about the shooting star. I kissed him back softly, and wrapped my arms around him underneath the blanket, running my hands over the girth of his arms. He gently nipped at my lower lip, and I sighed in pleasure before resting my head back on Linc's shoulder.

A flicker of movement on the beach caught my eye. I turned to look, squinting into the darkness, and saw there was something wiggling on the sand in the distance, about halfway between where we were and the breaking waves.

"Psst," I said quietly, to get Linc's attention.

"What is it?" he whispered back. I pointed in the direction where I saw the movement. Linc stood, and then helped me up, and hand in hand we crept closer to whatever it was. After just a few steps, I felt Linc squeeze my hand. He indicated a spot slightly to the left of the first wiggle I had seen.

"Another one."

"What are they, though?" I asked.

"Dunno, let's get closer," Linc said with the excited smile of a little boy.

When we were about six feet away from where the first wiggle had come from, I heard Linc gasp. "Look! There's hundreds of them!" He waved his hand at the expanse of sand in between us and the water.

A bright moonbeam shone off a shiny, flat appendage flapping off the side of one of the little creatures. Its back looked rounded, but it was generally shaped like a disk. I suddenly realized what we were looking at. Apparently so did Linc because we turned to each other at the same time. "Baby sea turtles?"

We both stared in amazement. The turtles were moving lightning fast for how small they were, determinedly flapping their flippers against the sand and creating rippled tracks behind them. In no time, the first one that I spotted had reached the water, pushing bravely ahead into the frothing waves, which, although small, must have seemed huge when seen through his little turtle eyes. A wave broke over him and he seemed to swim peacefully off.

"This is *incredible*," Linc said. "I've never known turtles to hatch at this time of the year or this far north. Their mother must have got lost. It's actually a miracle. "I have to go get Cole so he can see this."

I nodded. "But make sure LuLu stays in the tent. I don't want her to disturb the babies on their journey."

"Good thinking," Linc said, and squeezed my hand again before he rushed back to the tent. I folded my arms in front of me and lowered my chin into the neck of my jacket to protect myself from the cold, but other than that I was rendered motionless, spellbound by the incredible synchronized migration of the turtles.

"I couldn't wake him. He and LuLu are dead to the world," I heard Linc say as he walked up behind me. He took a step closer to me and wrapped his arms around me from behind, resting his chin on top of my head.

"I guess it's just for us to see then," I said, feeling special that Linc and I got to share the sight with each other. Realizing it was the middle of the night by then, I told Linc, "Let me know when you want to go back to the tent."

"Are you kidding? I don't want to miss a second of this." Pressing my back closer to him, I felt another rush of warmth as I relished in the comfort of his body against mine.

However, no matter how wonderful this moment with Linc was, I couldn't help but worry about how long it could last.

Chapter 9 - Linc

By the end of January, we had spent almost every day together. Either taking strolls with Cole, or simply watching movies or some documentary Cole or Shawn was interested in. He was a natural with kids, and I loved that he was taking special interest in Cole.

On one particularly walk, Cole had shifted back and forth in front of him, darting into the woods and then back out again as a wolf, turning back into a human to tell Shawn what he'd seen in the undergrowth. Shawn had sounded genuinely fascinated every time Cole relayed a detail about a dead bug or a cool tree root system he'd seen, and I loved him for it.

When Shawn had to work awkward hours, I'd drive to the hospital and bring him lunch or a cappuccino on my way to a job. By the second week, I was even getting used to the hospital smell, and I almost *liked* the faint scent of it on his clothes. He went out of his way to visit me on site on his way home from work most days, and had actually spent half of one of his days off with me as I installed a kitchen. It felt like time was speeding up every time we were together, and then slowed down to an agonizing crawl whenever we were apart.

The night before the full moon, I stopped at Nicole's to help her prepare some food for the pack run, though I spent most of the time leaning on her kitchen bench and talking about Shawn while she chopped vegetables.

"He seems hesitant," I admitted. "But I think it's because he's been hurt in the past."

"That's sad. What happened?"

"He's infertile, but that doesn't bother me, I don't need another kid."

"Would be nice though, huh? A cub with your fated mate?"

"Sure," I agreed, trying not to think about it. "But what I mean is, he's been hurt in the past *because* he's infertile. His last major relationship was with an alpha who blamed him when they couldn't get pregnant."

"Hm." She stopped chopping but kept looking at her knife. "I wonder if that's something the claiming bite would fix..."

"Let's not go there. It would be cruel to Shawn to mention the possibility. And who knows if I'll even get to claim him, especially if he feels too scared to commit?"

"You just need to show him that you're all-in. Just be consistent." She shrugged and went back to chopping.

"Well that's something I can do," I said, confidently.

***

The next morning, Shawn had the day off and we spent it together in town, browsing the boutiques and eating at our favorite cafes. He was yawning over his iced chai frappe and finally admitted he was tired, so we wandered back to his house and fell into bed for a "nap" that ended up being two quick hand jobs and a long snuggle. We were laying together with sheets tangled around our legs as the sun began to set.

"I have to get going soon or I'll be late for the full moon run," I said just before I kissed him.

He grumbled and pulled me into a tight hug, pushing his face against my neck. "Okay, I guess you better get going."

I chuckled as he gave no indication of letting me leave. I kissed the side of his face, and then squeezed him so hard he *had* to let me go so he could breathe. He laughed and ran a hand over my face.

"I'll see you tomorrow?" I asked, taking his hand and kissing his palm.

"I have work," he said, sighing. "I finish at seven. Dinner?"

"Yes," I said, kissing his lips again before dragging myself out of the bed.

"Are you, uh…" He waved his hand around like he was trying to find the words. "I mean, does anyone get hurt?"

"On the run?" I raised my eyebrows at him as I grabbed my pants off the floor.

"Yeah." He sat up and pulled the sheets up to his chest.

"No, my love." I bent down and kissed his forehead. "It doesn't hurt."

"What doesn't hurt?" he asked, frowning.

"Uh… shifting? From human form into wolf form. That's what you were asking about, right?"

Shawn shook his head and looked at me with wide eyes. "No, I meant… Do you…hunt?"

"Oh!" I let out a quick laugh. "You're asking if we hunt down poor defenseless animals?"

"Yeah, that's what I'm asking," he said, pulling the sheet higher and looking genuinely worried.

"Are you worried that we go crazy under the light of the moon and run into town and…bite unsuspecting nurses?" I pounced on top of Shawn and he let out a squeal as he tried to pull the sheet up over his face, but not before I got my mouth on his neck and gently bit down on the skin there. He squealed with laughter and kicked his legs, flailing and trying to kick me off. I pinned him down and pulled my face back to give him an innocent smile. He beamed at me and then quickly scowled.

"I'm *serious*!" he hissed.

"No, We don't bite anybody unless they want to be bitten."

"Why would anyone *want* to be bitten?" he asked, half trying to throw me off him.

I didn't budge. Instead, I cleared my throat. "It's how we can turn humans into wolf shifters."

Shawn suddenly went still, looking at me as if I'd suddenly gone mad, even more so than when I'd told him I was a shifter. "What?"

"There's a ritual that involves a bite," I said, keeping my voice calm. "It generally only happens between mates, and it's kind of like a wedding… Shifters who have human mates can bite them to claim them, to bring them into the pack." I swallowed nervously and watched Shawn's face for his reaction. He wasn't giving anything away, other than his shock. "Does that, uh…make sense?"

"No, at least, not scientifically. Not anatomically. Is there a blood borne virus involved? What makes a wolf shifter able to contort their body like that with no permanent damage? Let alone a *human* being able to do that?"

I chuckled and shook my head. "I wish I had answers for you. That stuff is way beyond me. I know the bite can also heal. Maybe we have stronger constitutions."

"What do you mean, *heal*?" Shawn asked, frowning at me.

"It can heal human diseases and stuff. If a human is sick, when they become a shifter, things just...get better. I mean, I don't know how. Jaxon has a bunch of medical books in his library you could look at, though."

"Medical books about wolf shifters?" he asked, squeezing my hands.

"You sound almost excited."

"I am! It's fascinating." He licked his lips and then asked, "Does the bite hurt?"

"I don't know for sure, but I'd guess it would... At least at first. I'll ask Bryce, if you like. Jaxon claimed him in the ritual I was talking about."

"Sure," he said, nodding. He looked like he was suddenly stuck in his head, thinking about something.

"Are you weirded out?" I asked, squeezing his hands.

"No. Strangely, I'm not. So, Bryce was human..."

"Yeah." I waited a few moments to see if Shawn was alright. He glanced at me, and then let go of my hands and motioned toward the door with a light smile.

"You're going to be late. It's already dark. Get out of here. Go run around the woods like a wild beast."

I laughed, and then kissed him once more before I grabbed my jacket and headed home.

***

The homestead was buzzing when I got there and the pack was already assembling beside the Wolf Lodge. Frankly, I was buzzing too. Introducing the idea of the claiming bite to Shawn had been easier than I'd expect, and I had to admit the idea made me feel downright excited. I was humming a sappy love song I'd heard on the local radio station as I bounded up to Jaxon where he was gathered with Gavin, Greer, and a group of other shifters.

"Lincoln!" Greer took my hand and immediately pulled me into a tight hug.

"Good to see you, Greer," I said.

He held me out at arm's length and beamed at me. "Jax tells me you've found yourself a lover."

"I didn't quite phrase it like that," Jaxon insisted.

"I think you said lover-boy," Greer said, teasing.

"Yeah, I've found someone pretty special. My mate."

Greer slapped my shoulder and congratulated me. "Human, right?"

I sighed and nodded, and then looked at Jaxon. "That's what I came to talk to Jax about, actually."

"It's time?" Jaxon asked quickly.

"I think so." I felt a little nervous being put on the spot. "Soon."

"Have you told him about the claiming bite?" Greer asked.

I nodded. "He seemed a little freaked out, but only a little. More fascinated than anything else."

"And you? How are you feeling about it?" Jaxon asked.

"I...love him," I admitted. My heart fluttered as I said the words out loud, and I felt my wolf whimper in frustration that our mate wasn't by our side for this run.

"But do you trust him?" Greer asked. I looked at him and found his face was set in concern. "And can you see yourself having a long life with him?"

"Yes, of course!" I said, feeling my wolf defensively get its hackles up.

"And a family?" Jaxon asked, looking right at me.

"Is this about his infertility?" I could have kicked myself for having confided in Nicole, but next to Jaxon she had always been my trusted confidant. She must have been really concerned to have mentioned it to Jaxon. Unless she thought he already knew. Jaxon nodded and the group frowned with uncertainty.

"C'mon, guys. I already have Cole, and he's a handful as it is. If we want more cubs down the road, we can always adopt."

The group, including Jaxon, shared a look of trepidation. It was in our nature to have children, and I suppose me saying I didn't necessarily want any more went against the pack's dynamics.

My wolf urged me to keep talking. "I love Shawn no matter what, even if he can't give me children, and it's good for the pack to bring in new shifters, even if we don't end up having more cubs. This is good for me, and it's good for all of us."

Jaxon looked at Greer who shrugged and nodded as if to say I was making perfect sense. After all, Jaxon had taken a human mate, and Greer himself had adopted Jaxon from shifters outside the pack when he was a baby.

"Do you want to make your intention official?" Jaxon asked, locking eyes with mine.

A small lump grew in my throat, suddenly nervous about making the declaration to Jaxon. But my wolf nudged me, and I swallowed dryly before officially stating, "I'm ready to make my claim on my mate, when he agrees to it."

Jaxon grinned at me proudly and embraced me as I smiled so hard I could barely contain myself.

"Congratulations, Linc," Gavin said as Greer nodded at me approvingly. Jaxon squeezed me hard and I practically popped in his grip. Laughing, I wrestled myself away and shoved him. He beamed at me and slapped my arm.

"We'll talk about the ceremony details soon, yeah?" he asked. Before I could give him an answer, he then turned to the pack and shouted, "Let's run!"

He let out a howl that set off the pack, then shifted and bounded through the crowd toward the woods. I stood with the rest of the group and watched as the pack took off, close on Jaxon's tail.

"What are you humming?" Gavin asked, a little oddly.

"Um. God, sorry," I groaned, not realizing I'd still had the song in my head. "Just a stupid love song I heard on the radio."

"I thought so," he said quietly. "On the nightly love songs and dedications show? With the DJ with that voice?"

"Uh... I guess?" I raised my eyebrows and cocked my head to the side as I nudged him playfully. "Do you regularly tune in to hear those sappy love songs?"

"No!" he growled, and then immediately shifted and sprinted off into the night. I let out a short laugh and followed him, bounding across the lawn on two clumsy legs before I shifted, fell to the ground, and burst through the brush on four paws.

***

The run gave me so much energy that I woke up before dawn. Cole had stayed at Nicole's, so the house was dead quiet. I switched on the radio and plodded around the cold, empty house with a cup of coffee. The same sappy love song came on and I fell onto the couch with a sigh, resting a hand on my heart and closing my eyes. I felt like I was on cloud nine.

Just as I was wondering when I'd next get to speak to Shawn, I felt my phone buzz in my pocket. It was Shawn. He must have been taking an early break. I couldn't help but let out a happy laugh, and I was still smiling as I answered. "Hey, gorgeous. What's happening?"

"Hey," he said, sounding weak. My wolf's ears pricked up a strain in his voice and I sat upright, suddenly worried.

"What's going on? Is everything alright?" I asked, quickly setting my coffee down on the table and standing up. I couldn't believe how hard my heart was racing.

"Everything's fine," he said, though his voice still sounded weary. "I'm just feeling really run down, and just... I don't feel good. At all. I can't work, but I don't think I should drive home."

"I'm on my way," I said, and immediately grabbed my keys and jacket.

I pulled up to the hospital and saw Shawn, looking pale and queasy, walking out from the front doors. I quickly parked, and then grabbed a blanket from the back of the truck before racing over to wrap it around his shoulders.

"Okay?" I asked, helping him over to the truck.

"I'm okay. You're sweet for picking me up."

"Don't mention it," I said as I opened the door. I helped him into the passenger seat before climbing back into the driver's side. My wolf started sniffing as soon I put my hand on Shawn's forehead. Neither of us could tell what was wrong, though. He felt warm, but I didn't think he had a fever.

"Did you talk to any of the doctors?" I asked as he rested his head back against the seat and closed his eyes.

Shawn nodded. "They said it was probably a bug that's going around. Stay warm, stay hydrated, lots of rest—you know, the usual."

"The usual, huh?" I turned on the engine and cranked up the heat. "Can I take you back to the homestead with me?"

"Hm? Is there some shifter cure for a stomach bug that modern medicine doesn't know about?" he asked, a little smirk edging on the side of his lips.

I chuckled. "There probably is, actually, but I just want to get you home so I can keep you warm, hydrated, and resting."

"I don't want to get Cole sick," he murmured.

"First of all, he's got wolf blood, he can fight off the worst infections. Second of all, he's at Nicole's and he'll be at school until this afternoon. Plus, I can keep you quarantined."

Shawn smiled a little, and then made a queasy face and let out a pained groan. "Alright. Take care of me. I feel rotten."

We stopped at Pampered Paws Doggie Daycare to pick up LuLu on our way.

"The owner is quite the character," Shawn said in warning before I reluctantly left him in the car with the motor running and the heat blasting.

As soon as I bounded into the shop, I found out he was right. The first thing I saw was a chubby red-headed man in an out of season, bright pink outfit. I don't mean fashionably out of season, I mean, he looked like he was dressed for the height of summer—short-sleeves, shorts and a visor. I blinked to clear my vision and found his smile was just as bright as the color of his outfit.

"Well, hello!" he said, his gaze flitting up and down my body.

"Hello," I replied. "I'm here to get LuLu, for Shawn."

"For Shawn, *hm*?" He squinted at me. "Shawn didn't say anything about a handsome alpha stopping by today to pick up his pride and joy."

"It's an unplanned pick-up. He's unwell," I explained, craning my neck to look past him to the back of the shop where I could hear dogs playing.

"Oh, poor darling!" the man said. "But I'm afraid I can't just let LuLu leave with a complete stranger." He glanced up and down my body again, and then scowled.

"I... I'm not a stranger."

The man kept scowling.

"Shawn and I are, uh, together. I'm Linc?" I said in question instead of a statement. This man was kind of intimidating to be honest.

"Oh! *Lincoln*! Well why didn't you say so," he said in a kind of purr. "I've heard so much about you. I'm Trevor. LuLu's favorite uncle. Welcome to my doggy daycare."

As we shook hands, I thought I caught a hint of knowing in his eyes, like he was detecting something secret about me. The guy was definitely a human, but I remembered Shawn telling me Trevor had mentioned shifters, and I wondered if he actually *knew*. Before I had decided to subtly question him, Trevor broke eye contact and peered over my shoulder toward the truck parked out the front of the shop.

"Is that our darling Shawn?"

I turned to follow his gaze and spotted Shawn looking downright miserable in the passenger seat.

"Oh gods!" Trevor exclaimed. "He looks ghastly! What's wrong with the poor thing?"

"Just a bug," I said.

"Mmhmmm..." Trevor looked me over suspiciously. "Well, you wait right here. I'll go get that corgi cutie for you."

I did as I was told and waited while he walked to the back of the shop. I heard a cacophony of excited dog barks as he opened the door to the daycare area, followed by him shushing everyone.

"Alright, where's that little LuLu? There she is! There she is! Come here, sweetie. Your dad's beau is here to pick you up."

I couldn't help but smile a little at the affection in his voice. The door reopened and LuLu trotted out on a long sparkly leash, wearing a bow-tie the same shade as Trevor's shirt. I looked from her, to him, and then back to her again.

"Listen," he said quietly. "Between you and me, she's been a little anxious these last few days. Some dogs like to play dress-up—it gives them permission to be a different dog for the day. The bow-tie gives LuLu a business-bitch attitude. No anxiety."

I raised my eyebrows and looked at LuLu. I had to admit, she did look confident...

"Any idea why she's been anxious?" I asked, kneeling down and giving her a pat hello. LuLu licked my hand, and then turned around so I would rub her rump.

"Beats me. She's not usually such a nervous nelly... Maybe something different happening at home, hm?"

I glanced up and caught an accusatory look on Trevor's face before he snapped on a sweet smile.

"You think she's anxious because I'm around?" I asked point-blank.

Trevor shrugged. "Could be. Could also be she's picked up on Shawn's illness. Dogs tend to detect these things before us humans do…"

"Right," I said, looking down at LuLu and wondering just how intuitive a corgi could be. Maybe I was underestimating her. Trevor gave LuLu some farewell treats and let her keep the bow-tie for the night. She hurried toward the car and tried to clamber over the backseat to crawl into Shawn's lap.

"Oh, Lu!" Shawn groaned, but gave her happy kisses. "My tummy doesn't feel so good, and it feels much worse with paws pressing against it."

"C'mon LuLu, stay in the backseat until we get home," I told her gently as I picked her up and got her settled in the back.

"Home…" I heard Shawn say under his breath with a little sigh.

I drove as smoothly as I could through town, slowing to nearly a stop to ease the car over the pothole on the corner of Pack Lane and Growling Oak Way. It took all of ten minutes to get to my house, but Shawn was already fast asleep by the time I pulled into the drive. I looked over at him as I turned off the car and watched for any signs of him stirring.

Not a peep.

I reached over and rested a hand on his thigh. He didn't rouse. I couldn't help but smile as I looked at his face, his parted lips, and his cheeks just a little flushed. My wolf was pacing back and forth. It didn't feel anxious like LuLu, just protective and at full attention.

I got LuLu out of the car as quietly as I could, but Shawn woke as soon as her paws hit the ground.

"Mm, how long was I out?" he asked, shrugging the blanket off his shoulders.

"Just the drive home, not long," I said, then opened up his door.

"I feel a little better," he said, smiling. He still looked—what had Trevor said? Ghastly. But before I had a chance to offer him a hand, he swung his legs out of the car and tumbled out, almost falling down.

"Oh!" he cried. I grabbed him around the waist and steadied him to his feet.

"Hold on to me," I said, wrapping his arm around my shoulder. "Are you sure this is just a bug?"

"I'm just dizzy. It happens," he said in dismissal. I wanted to believe him, so I didn't argue as we walked together into the house.

I got Shawn set up on the couch in the living room with piles of blankets. He insisted that he stay in a room with a door so he didn't spread germs through the house.

"Wolf medicine?" he asked with a cheeky grin as I handed him a cup of tea.

"Sure, if that gives you the placebo effect you need to feel better."

He took a sip and moaned in appreciation. "Tastes just like human lemon and ginger tea."

"Oh really? Funny…" I said, and grinned.

Shawn dozed on and off, and LuLu stayed by his side as I built us a fire. Once that was roaring, I tottered back and forth from the kitchen with more tea while also cooking him up a big pot of vegetable soup. Eventually he fell into a deep sleep, so I took advantage of the moment to walk in the woods and collect some wild mushrooms, which I then added to the pot as it simmered on the stove.

"What's that smell?" Cole exclaimed as he bounded in through the kitchen door and threw his school bag on the dining table.

"Dinner," I said, ruffling his hair as he scooted past and opened the fridge. "Shawn's here and—"

"Shawn! Awesome! I want to show him what I did to my telescope, he's going to think it's so cool!"

"*Shh*, quiet please—he's sleeping. He's sick."

"It's four in the afternoon!" Cole raised his arms out at all directions.

"He's sick," I repeated.

Cole pouted and let his arms drop.

"Close the fridge, kiddo," I said. "Homework before dinner. Then you can do star research."

He pouted even harder and made a show of closing the fridge very slowly and very quietly, and then tip-toed up the stairs to his room. He came back down a couple of hours later, already sleepy-eyed and hungry for dinner.

"Can I set a place for Shawn, just in case he's feeling better?" he asked quietly, holding up a spoon and a napkin.

"You can, but I don't think he'll be up for eating at the table yet." Just then, the living room door creaked open.

"Oh, I'm up," Shawn said with a smile.

"Did you wake up because of the smell?" Cole giggled and held his nose.

Shawn laughed briefly then caught my stern scowl and cut it short. "Well, it does smell quite medicinal in here," Shawn said in defense of Cole, and I couldn't help but smile. "I guess if we're eating such nutritious soup then I shouldn't be worried about spreading my germs."

"Cole has a very strong immune system." I made the comment while ladling out big bowls of the thick soup, really loving the banter between Shawn and Cole. They got on so well I could really see us living together as a family.

"I'm basically a superhero," Cole said as he took his seat and smiled at Shawn.

"Hm, I suppose that's actually quite true." Shawn took a seat opposite Cole, and LuLu trotted over to sit at his feet. "You do have some pretty impressive powers."

"Thanks. I've never been sick."

"Are you kidding?" Shawn asked, sounding genuinely suspicious.

I shook my head as I placed bowls in front of them. "Maybe a couple of sniffles, but I'm telling you—shifter immune systems are insane."

"Insane," Cole mimicked, and took a slurp of soup before making a grossed-out face that I willfully ignored.

"I need to get my hands on those medical books of Jaxon's," Shawn said, blowing on his spoonful.

We ate together and I was impressed that Cole respectfully kept his star-gazing questions to a minimum. I kept a close eye on Shawn, and so did my wolf, sensing that something was still off even though he was looking much better with brighter eyes and a bit more color in his face.

After Cole somehow managed to choke down his bowl of mushroom-rich soup, I tucked him into bed. LuLu tottered in behind me and stopped at the doorway of the lamp-lit room.

Glowing stars, arranged in patterns of actual constellations, covered Cole's walls and gave the timber room an eerie alien color.

"Come up here, LuLu," Cole whispered, sleepily patting the spot next to him. The corgi jumped up without hesitation and nuzzled in close to Cole. He draped an arm over his side and cuddled her, placing his book on the pillow where they could both see it. LuLu still wore her bow-tie and Cole adjusted it so it was out of the way as she lay her head with a heavy sigh.

I gave Cole a kiss goodnight and patted LuLu, and then eased out of the room and left the door open ajar. I hesitated for a moment to look back at the scene and felt my wolf frolic with excitement at how our family was growing. I bit down on my bottom lip as I took the stairs two at a time to get back to the living room as quickly as possible. That's where I found Shawn sitting on the couch and gazing into the fire with the blankets bunched up beside him. I leaped over the back of the sofa and landed next to him with a thud.

He gasped and clutched his chest in surprise, and then let out a laugh. "You are fast!"

"I can be." I wiggled my eyebrows. "I missed you. How are you feeling?" I pressed my hand against his forehead, and he leaned against it as he sighed.

"Much better. Still kind of queasy, but the soup actually really helped."

"I wish I could just heal you. I'm not used to human frailty. I wish I could give you some of those superhero powers Cole was talking about," I said with a bit of cheek.

Shawn chuckled and then moved closer to me. I took him into my arms and he lay against my chest. We sat gazing at the fire, in deep silence until he whispered, "I wish you could too."

My wolf surged. I looked down at the top of Shawn's head and planted a soft kiss there before I asked him what he meant. "You wish I could…"

"I wish you could…change me."

Those had to be the sweetest words I'd ever heard. I hardly believed it. Shawn wanted to be a wolf? My own wolf dashed back and forth with so much excitement it felt like my whole body was vibrating. I took slow, quiet breaths, determined to take it slow and steady. Shawn fell silent, and I was left with a deep yearning. It was uncomfortable, how much I wanted to claim him. Hell, it was almost unbearable.

"Shawn…"

"Mm?" He craned his neck to look up at me.

"I love you," I whispered.

A bright smile burst across his face and his eyes pricked with tears. "Oh, Linc. I love you too."

I bit my bottom lip in an effort to stop myself from racing ahead, but my mouth felt like it had words jammed in there, which I just needed to get out. "Do you remember when I told you about the claiming bite?" I asked as quietly as I could manage.

"You think I would forget something that crazy?"

I laughed and shook my head. "Is it crazy?"

"Uh, yeah. It's crazy," he said. My heart was sinking before he added, "But it's also kind of cool."

I smiled to myself and took a bracing breath. It was now or never. "I'd like to claim you… If you wanted me to."

Shawn fell silent. I felt his body tense, and his breathing became shallow.

"We don't have to. I didn't mean to pressure you, if this isn't something you want. I understand how scary it sounds, with the bite and all..."

"No it's not that," he said, turning to look away. "I just don't know why... I mean... Are you sure?"

I moved, encouraging him to look up at me. He did so reluctantly, meeting my eyes. His tears started to well over.

"I'm not sure why you'd want to do that, when I can't give you kids."

"Shawn... I want to claim you as you are. Kids or not. I want to so badly," I insisted, staring into his eyes. "Please believe me."

He swallowed, and then looked away for a moment before sitting up and facing me. "Honestly, Linc, this is going really fast."

My wolf whined, and I felt myself backing up, bracing myself against the inevitable let-down.

"Really fast," he said again, before he broke out in a huge grin. "And I like it. I've never felt like this before. I've never been so happy. Did you just...kind of propose to me?"

I laughed and nodded. "I guess I did. Sorry I don't have a ring or something, it's not really customary..."

Shawn shook his head. "No need." He paused for a moment and took my hands as he wet his lips. I watched as his gaze dragged over my face, and then he softly whispered, "Yes."

"Yes?" My voice wavered in disbelief. "Yes?"

"Yes! Yes, yes, yes! Make me into a freakin' wolf, I don't care, I want to be with you, I want to be part of your family, your *pack*, the whole lot. Yes!"

My wolf pranced in joyous relief, and I enfolded Shawn in my arms. I couldn't stop smiling. I had no words. I planted kisses all over his face.

"So, uh, sooner is better. Maybe it'll get rid of this gross bug," he said.

Yes, you're right. Sooner better than later." I held him at arm's length and gazed at his beautiful face. "Wait right here. I'll call Jaxon and get started on organizing the ceremony."

"Now?"

"I can't wait. Don't move."

"I won't," he promised, then he took my hands and kissed them as he gazed deep into my eyes.

I'd left my phone in my jacket pocket when I'd gone out earlier to pick the mushrooms, so I headed to the kitchen. I stood at the counter, phone in hand, and through the kitchen window, I noticed the clear night sky and how the moon was still shockingly bright and full. I could also see the wood shed covered in frost, glittering like diamonds in the freezing air.

"It's on. Shawn wants me to claim him," I told Jaxon the second he answered, barely containing the joy in my voice. Silence hung on the end of the line and my heart ached for a moment. Had I moved too fast? Had he expected Shawn to say *no*? Was he worried about Shawn's fertility?

"Congratulations, Linc!"

"Great news!" I heard Bryce call out in the background, followed by the wail of a crying baby.

"Ah, shit, sorry—I'll step outside," Jaxon said.

"So, when do you want to have the ceremony?"

"As soon as possible. Do you think within the next couple of days will be too soon?"

"Not my end, but won't Shawn want some say in vows etc. I know Bryce wanted something like a wedding even though us shifters don't actually get married. I'm assuming Shawn might want something like that too. I'd ask him first, Linc, but whenever it suits you, we can get it done."

"Thanks…" I was about to add more, when I started to feel something tugging inside me.

"What's wrong?" Jaxon asked. It didn't surprise me Jaxon knew there was something not quite right just then.

"My wolf is sensing something…strange. It's kind of throwing me. I don't know, I feel ultra-protective all of a sudden."

"Hm, well… You said Shawn's sick. It's normal to feel protective. Keep an eye on it, though."

"Sure," I said. "Hm, I wonder if—"

A howl pierced the air. Unlike anything I'd heard from a wolf. It wasn't coming from outside either. I quickly spun on my heel and dashed back to the living room, following the sound.

I hung up on Jaxon without thought, and just as I entered the living room, the howls turned to barks. My heart stopped. LuLu yapped loudly and pawed at Shawn before letting out another pint-sized howl. Shawn's body lay limp on the floor, eyes open, staring up at the ceiling. He wasn't moving.

"Fuck!" My wolf frantically clawed at my chest as I rushed over. I dropped to the floor beside Shawn and desperately searched for his pulse.

"No, no, no! C'mon! *Fuck*!"

Finally, I felt a faint thudding against my fingertips as I pressed them against his neck. "Oh thank god." I slapped Shawn's cheek gently. "C'mon, Shawn! Wake up!"

No response. LuLu whimpered and pawed anxiously at his side.

"Fuck." I scampered back and found my phone on the floor where I'd dropped it. Without hesitation, I dialed nine-one-one.

"I need an ambulance," I cried the second an operator answered. The operator started asking me questions as they sent the ambulance, but I was too wound up to answer them properly.

"I don't know, I don't know! He's a nurse. I don't know his medical history! He's been nauseous and dizzy today, that's all I know, and now he's unconscious. I don't know. I don't know. Please just hurry!"

Chapter 10 - Shawn

Hovering between sleep and waking, I felt like I was floating in a dark pool. I was buoyant, but lost, with no stars or sight of land to guide me. I strained all my senses trying to get any idea of where I was. Then slowly, light began to dawn and reach my eyes. I saw soft orange light, fuzzy shapes, and a collection of shadows. Maybe a line of trees? I blinked a few times and the blurred scene came into slightly sharper focus. The trees were people. They were gathered around me, but I didn't recognize any of them.

Panic began to build in my chest, but I tried to tamp it down, knowing it wouldn't do me any good.

"Shawn?"

A familiar voice. I closed my eyes again, trying to place it.

"Shawn, can you hear me?"

I opened my eyes and saw a handsome man, with beautiful toffee-colored eyes, looking at me with both concern and warmth. With love.

I definitely recognized him.

"Linc!"

"Oh, Shawn, thank god." Linc gently placed his palm on my cheek. "Are you okay?"

I smiled weakly, then asked myself the same question, panic rising once again. "I...don't know." I looked around at the other people in the room. I saw an EMT badge on one of them. "Am I?"

"Can you tell me your name?" the paramedic asked.

"Shawn... Shawn Drocella," I answered hoarsely.

"Great. And do you know where you are?"

"I'm..." I didn't want to cry as fear pumped adrenalin through my veins, but then I heard the crackling fire in the wood burner, and my fear subsided.

"I'm in Linc's living room," I answered, relief making me smile as I looked back at Linc. His expression was tense and worried as he held one of my hands in both of his.

"I'm so glad you're okay, my love," Linc said, kissing my palm again.

The paramedic who first spoke to me, did so again. "We're going to get you to the hospital, Shawn. They'll do some more tests when we get there so we can find out what happened and make sure you're feeling one hundred percent."

"Mm, okay," I mumbled. I felt so crushingly tired now the shock of waking up on the floor had worn off.

"I'll be right there with you the whole way," Linc said, squeezing my hand.

"Wait, what about Cole and LuLu?" I asked, suddenly remembering it wasn't just me Linc was responsible for. "We can't leave them alone!" I felt my pulse quicken, and I started to feel lightheaded again.

"Nicole is on her way over to pick them up," Linc assured me. "All you need to worry about is getting better."

"Okay, that sounds...fine." I relaxed again and put my heavy head back down on the floor.

***

The ambulance ride was a blur. Once I was wheeled into a room in the emergency department, a flurry of paramedics and nurses peppered me with questions, filling in my chart and taking my vitals again.

"I'm going to take some blood so we can run tests, alright Shawn?" one of the nurses, a pretty brunette I recognized from work, asked me.

"Sure, that's fine," I said.

"I guess I already know you're a pro with needles. You work in L&D, right?"

I nodded. "I've seen you around..." I tried to see if I remembered her name. "Paloma, right?"

"That's right," she said, flashing a brilliant smile. "Impressive, for someone in your state."

"Thanks," I said with a weak smile.

"Well, you already know we'll take very good care of you. We have only the best of the best quality nurses at *this* hospital," Paloma said as she prepped the tourniquet and syringe. I chuckled softly, but when she started to pull blood out of my arm, my lightheadedness came back.

"*Oooof*, I don't feel so good," I said quietly. Linc rushed closer to me, then leaned in and kissed my forehead.

"Squeeze my hand," he said. I did, hard.

"All done!" Paloma declared. "Sorry about that. It didn't hurt too bad, did it?"

"No, no," I assured her. "I just started feeling dizzy and a bit queasy again."

"Okay, well you sit tight. The doctor will be in in a minute." She turned to Linc. "You come get me if anything happens, I'll be right over at the nurse's station."

"Thank you so much, I will," Linc said, exhaling rapidly.

I didn't know Linc's devotion and thoughtfulness could get even more intense than it had been so far. Now I was ill, he seemed eager to rise to the task of caring for me. Whenever I was sick, Phillip treated me like a leper and an inconvenience. He was always worried about catching whatever I had. I was truly in a whole new world of romance with Linc.

"I know this might not be the best time, but I'm just so relieved you're okay, and I'm wondering, does this change how you feel about the claiming ceremony?" he asked in a whisper.

"No. Definitely not. I still want to do it," I answered, relieved he still wanted to claim me. "I think we better find out what's wrong with me first, though."

"Of course, of course," Linc said, clearly relieved as well. "We can postpone it as long as we need to."

"Hello, Shawn," I heard a familiar voice say as someone pulled open the curtain.

"Dr. Shah, hi," I said, recognizing the staff doctor immediately.

"How are you feeling?"

"I'm okay now. The nausea keeps coming and going."

"Well, that makes sense, considering. I have some news," he said, cautiously looking between Linc and me.

"What is it?" Linc asked, a hint of panic in his voice.

Dr. Shah looked back at Linc, then me again, his expression stoic. "Is this your partner, Shawn?"

"It is, and I give you permission to talk to me about my health in his presence."

"Very professional," Dr. Shah said before he smiled. "Well, Shawn... You're pregnant."

I stared at Dr. Shah's face. I noticed he had a thick, black moustache I didn't remember seeing on him last time we crossed paths at the hospital.

"Did you...grow out a moustache?" I asked him.

Dr. Shah looked puzzled, then concerned. I felt Linc's hand clutching tightly to mine, but I was still staring at the doctor as if he'd gone a little mad, or I had.

"Shawn, did you hear me?" he asked, raising his voice slightly. "I said you're pregnant."

"That... Um, no. That can't be right," I said, my pulse quickening to the point I felt dizzy again. I turned to Linc and grasped his forearm tightly, my fingernails pressing into his skin. "I'm infertile. I can't have children."

Dr. Shah cocked his head slightly to the side, and in a perfunctory tone said, "It seems you're incorrect about that, Shawn."

"This is impossible," I insisted. I looked at Linc. He shook his head, his disbelief evident in the widening of his eyes.

"Are you *positive*?" Linc asked the doctor.

"I haven't been wrong in fifteen years of pregnancy tests," Dr. Shah said matter-of-factly.

If I was pregnant, then did that mean all this time I've been mourning my inability to have a child and it wasn't even my fault? That scumbag! That asshole! I clenched my jaw as I thought of all the things I wanted to call Phillip. I couldn't believe he'd made me feel so worthless, so wretched, for *years*, just because he didn't want to admit he could be the one who was infertile.

"Oh my god..." I said as it finally dawned on me. I was pregnant! I turned to Linc and saw he seemed to be in the same state of shock as me. There were tears brimming in his eyes.

"The nausea and light headedness. I can't believe I didn't realize it sooner, but why would I? I mean... I didn't think..." I looked back at Dr. Shah.

He smiled awkwardly. "Just a very bad case of morning sickness, which as you know can last all day," he stated. "I'll send you home with some recommendations for some home remedies and prenatal vitamins," he added, writing something in his chart. "So, congratulations." He smiled and gave us a thumbs up before leaving the room.

Congratulations? Should I be congratulated? I couldn't process the maelstrom of emotions I was caught up in—positive, negative, and everything in between.

Linc seemed like he was still in shock, looking at me with a furrowed brow. That's when I started to panic.

What if he doesn't want a baby? What if he thought me being infertile was a good thing and this is all a horrible mistake to him? He never actually said he wanted a baby. Maybe Cole had always been enough for him! What if this scares him away? What if he abandons me just like Phillip did? Fertile or infertile, maybe I just can't be loved by anyone... My heart rate became irregular, and though I tried to take slow and even breaths, the room seemed to darken.

"Linc?" I said desperately, attempting to prompt a response from him. He just stared at me with wide eyes, shaking his head again.

"Can you *please* say something?"

"I don't know what to say," Linc said.

"Anything! Please. How do you *feel?*"

Linc slowly raised his hands to my face and placed one on each of my cheeks. I felt my lips trembling as I continued to frantically search his face for any indication of joy or anger.

"Shawn…" He said my name slowly, as if not sure what it was he wanted to say. "I've never been…"

"You've never been *what?*" I demanded.

"So happy in my entire life." His face erupted into a radiant grin.

"Neither have I," I admitted as Linc leaned in to kiss me. He pressed his lips against mine with such love I could feel it in my toes. When I pulled back it was so I could take a much needed breath.

"We're having a *baby,*" Linc whispered to me. We broke out in laughter, and Linc wrapped me up in his arms, hugging me gently.

"We're going to be a family. A real family," I said, unable to believe it.

"There's no one I'd rather do this with," Linc replied.

I felt the shockwaves of the news reverberating through my chest. It felt like the whole room was vibrating. Linc let go of our embrace and pulled over a chair so he could sit next to me and hold my hand.

"This is crazy," I said. "I told you I was infertile, didn't I?"

Linc nodded. "Yes, and I told you I didn't mind."

"Phillip and I tried so many times. And nothing ever came of it," I explained, sniffling as I tried to reconcile my new future with how I'd always thought it would be.

"I guess it was him after all. Or maybe something else. But it's definitely not you, my love. Clearly," Linc said with a chuckle.

"Clearly…" I said dreamily.

"Maybe you were just waiting for your fated mate," he suggested with a smirk.

I chuckled then looked at him with a tired grin. I shook my head. There was no way to make sense of it; how this had all come to be, but I was beginning to see how wonderful it all was.

***

Once the hospital released me, Linc took me back to his place where we could both relax knowing I wasn't sick or contagious. Linc got me set up to rest in bed. He lent me some of his clothes—a pair of sweatpants that were conveniently loose, and a baggy tee shirt. He piled every blanket in the house on his bed, placed a glass of water and a cup of tea on the bedside table, and to top it off, offered to give me a massage.

"Well, I'm not going to say no to *that,*" I said with certainty.

Linc pulled off my socks and started massaging my feet. He dug his thumb into the arch of my foot, and I felt a pleasant aching reverberate up my leg.

"A *foot* massage? Wow, I didn't know I could be any happier about being pregnant."

Linc just smiled and kept rubbing the arch of my foot, then leaned down and kissed each of my toes.

"Mm, that feels amazing," I said, leaning my head back on the pile of pillows Linc had arranged for me.

"I love that you're pregnant," Linc said, slowly kissing his way up my foot now, toward my ankle. He kept planting tiny kisses, slowly moving over my ankle. He pushed up the leg of my pants and started kissing his way up my shin. "I love the fact you got pregnant the first time we had sex."

"I still can't believe it. I'm having a baby! *Your* baby."

"*Our* baby," he said, crawling up the bed toward me.

"*Our* baby," I repeated with a contented sigh.

Linc heaved his bulky chest over mine and lifted one hand off the bed to stroke my cheek.

"I love you," he said, and kissed me on the mouth.

"I love you too, you handsome wolf," I said with a giggle.

"You think my wolf is handsome?" Linc asked, waggling his eyebrows.

"Yeah, I do, actually. I prefer you as a human, though."

"*Aaaa-ooooh!*" Linc let out a playful howl, then fell on top of me, laughing.

I reached up to pull his face to mine and kissed him passionately. He moaned into my mouth, and then slid his hand beneath my tee shirt. It was my turn to moan. I loved the way he touched me—soft yet demanding. I tugged at his shirt and pulled it off him. Grinning, Linc stripped me of mine, and then we returned to hungry kissing. I felt the familiar hazy high of being with him; a strange cocktail of chemicals he invoked in me swirling around my bloodstream. The pregnancy hormones seemed to add a mellowing effect as well, making me feel floppy and dazed.

Linc took the opportunity to pamper me, kissing all the way down my neck and across my collarbones, swirling his tongue around my left nipple while he twisted the other in his fingers. I lay back and groaned. Linc switched his mouth to my right nipple, sending electric currents shooting to my balls. With another groan I arched my spine and scraped my fingernails along the thick muscles of his back, spurring him on. He quickly looked up at me, his eyes bright with lust before he began licking my stomach and kissing his way to the loose waistband of his sweatpants that had pooled on my hips. He wiggled his tongue under the elastic, teasing me and making me squirm before he slid the sweatpants off of me.

Staring down my body, I held my breath as Linc, so very softly, pressed his lips to the head of my cock before taking it into his mouth.

"Linc, that feels so good," I whispered, almost afraid to speak aloud in case he stopped. He chuckled, and then sucked, gently yet forcefully. Pleasure combined with need swirled around my chest and stomach. I tried to hold back on crying out, on shoving my cock all the way down his throat, but Linc practically did it for me, sinking deeper and then swallowing.

"Oh god." I watched him, my alpha, sucking me off with obvious enjoyment if his soft moans were anything to go by. He gripped the base of my shaft and started pumping my cock in time with the movements of his hot, wet mouth. It didn't take long before I felt my balls aching, tight and full against my body.

"Coming," I mumbled, not sure if I was warning Linc or pleading with him. Linc moaned in response and kept sliding his soft lips along my shaft. Tingles radiated throughout my body— my dick as the epicenter. Linc cupped my balls in his hand while he sucked me just a little harder. I'm sure I ripped Linc's sheets as dug my fingers into them, desperate to come yet desperate to hold off for as long as possible, but the way he flicked his tongue over the slit of my cock was too much. I couldn't stop the flash of intense pleasure that tore through me. Nor could I stop my strained cry as my cock spewed cum straight down Linc's throat. He eagerly sucked and swallowed it all down, and then sighed and smiled in satisfaction.

"Okay?" he asked as he crawled up to sweetly kiss my mouth.

"Mm." I don't think I had the strength to say anything else. Linc grinned then lay down beside me, pulling me to him so I could rest within the circle of his arms.

I breathed in his scent. Clean, male, aroused. I groaned and lifted my face to kiss the racing pulse at the side of his neck. Slick trickled from my ass, and even though I'd just come I wanted him inside me, where he belonged.

"Linc, make love to me."

At his soft smile it occurred to me how fortunate I was. Until now I had never believed anything like this would be possible. Not for me. I thought I'd have to settle for being childless, for never finding someone to love me besides LuLu. I loved her, but I had to admit I was getting real lonely before I met Linc. And now? Now I had a family and was joining a community that felt like home. All the dreams I dared to have were coming true, and I honestly never felt happier.

Chapter 11 - Linc

"Daddy-to-be, coming through!" Gavin called out as he pushed through the small group of adult shifters who had assembled around a bonfire at the back of Jaxon's house.

I laughed and rolled my eyes as I let myself be dragged by the sleeve of my jacket. "I'm already a dad," I said as a reminder.

"Baby-daddy-to-be, coming through!" Gavin corrected himself and chuckled at his own joke as we approached a circle of alphas. I tried to scowl at him, but I couldn't stop myself from beaming. It had been two weeks since we'd found out Shawn was pregnant, and I still felt lightheaded and giggly every time I was reminded of it.

"Hey, it's the super dad!" Jaxon said with a laugh. The alphas greeted me with hugs and slaps on the back.

"Now, what's going on with the claiming ceremony?" Jaxon asked, handing me a mug of hot chocolate as I sat between him and Greer on a large log in front of the fire. "I haven't heard a peep from you for days."

"That's actually what I want to talk to you about," I said, my voice taking on a somber tone. "Does anybody know what the effects are on a pregnant human?"

"The effects of the bite?" Gavin asked, then glanced at Greer.

"Well, just the usual. They're turned but can't shift until they've had the baby," Greer said.

"But what about complications? Has anyone heard of anything adverse happening?" I asked.

"Bryce was pregnant with Lori when I bit him, and everything was fine," Jaxon replied.

"I know, but how often has that happened, that a human receives the claiming bite while pregnant? Do we have any other instances in recent memory?"

Jaxon frowned. "Actually, I think Bryce was the first pregnant human to be claimed in quite some time."

"Then I can't take the risk without knowing. Just because Bryce was alright doesn't mean Shawn will be."

"I can understand your concern," Greer said. "But I've honestly never heard of anything bad happening."

"Sorry, but that's not good enough." I shook my head. This wasn't what I wanted to hear, and my protective instincts kicked in again. I would not take a chance on anything happening to Shawn or the baby. No way.

"Speak with Dr. Reed," Jaxon said. "She's been the pack's obstetrician for years, I'm sure she'll know."

"Yeah, that's a good idea." I nodded, a little relieved someone would have a professional answer.

"And in the meantime, what about the ceremony?" Gavin asked.

"The last thing I want to do is to postpone it, but I'm not going to claim Shawn until I'm sure both he and the baby will be safe."

Jaxon looked disappointed but put a hand on my shoulder for support. Greer and Gavin both nodded in agreement. Now I just needed to break the news to Shawn.

***

The next day, I picked Cole up from school and headed straight for Shawn's house.

"Isn't it my weekend at Mom's?" Cole asked before he even got buckled up.

"Yeah, she'll pick you up from Shawn's later," I explained again—for the third time that day.

"But should I go home to get my telescope in case Shawn wants to look at stars together?" he asked, looking out of the window distractedly.

"We're already late, Cole. And I'm sure you can both share his telescope." I made a motion with my hand that said I needed him to hurry the hell up with the seatbelt.

"Oh yeah!" he said, smiling brightly. "Maybe I can use his!"

Just like magic, he quickly buckled up and kicked his legs excitedly, making up a song about some star constellations I'd never heard of as I drove us across town. This was the night Shawn and I had decided to tell Cole about the baby. We hadn't told him earlier because we were taking the time to absorb it ourselves. I knew Shawn was over the moon about having a baby, but I wondered if he was okay about having one with *me*. There were small moments when I worried he'd simply agreed to be my mate because he hadn't considered having children, and now we were having one together, did he think I was a good enough alpha to raise our kids? The only thing he had to go one was the way I'd raised Cole. I'd tried, of course, but not every parent had all the answers, and I'm sure there may have been something Shawn thought I'd done wrong. Was that enough for him not to want me? Would he change his mind after the baby was born?

As I navigated the streets of Timberwood Cove I tried not to allow my fears to take away what should be a time of happiness, but with my worry about the claiming bite and what it would do to Shawn and the baby, I wasn't exactly jumping for joy right now. On top of that, I'd yet to tell Shawn about postponing it until we'd spoken to Dr. Reed. I sighed as I pulled up into the drive of Shawn's house, worried about how the next few hours were going to go.

As Cole and I walked up to Shawn's front door, it flew open to reveal LuLu wearing her special bowtie and Shawn in a handsome navy-blue sweater. God the man was gorgeous.

"That was fast," I said in surprise.

"LuLu heard you coming," Shawn explained before kissing me quickly. As we parted, I looked down and saw LuLu jumping in happy circles around Cole who was laughing and jumping in return.

"She's still into the bowtie?" I asked.

"I guess she's still nervous about the you-know-what," Shawn whispered, then motioned for us to get inside. "Come in, come in, it's freezing."

Shawn had already told me he'd made pizza dough, so as we entered his kitchen we got straight to work to build our own pizzas. Cole loved stacking his base with way too many toppings, and Shawn did a great job of secretly picking a few of them off so it ended up evenly cooked and actually kind of tasty.

We ate at the table, and as Cole took a bite of his second slice, I cleared my throat and got his attention.

"What?" he asked with his mouth stuffed with pizza.

"Don't talk with your mouth full," I told him.

"I wasn't until you looked at me and coughed," he said after he'd swallowed his mouthful.

I laughed. "Sorry, kiddo. I just wanted to get your attention."

"That's okay," he said happily and gave me a big cheesy grin.

I glanced at Shawn, suddenly feeling like I was totally on the spot, and not quite sure how to proceed. He gave me an encouraging smile and nodded at me, as if to say he knew I had it in me.

"So, we have something important to tell you. Do you think this is a good time to talk about it or would you like to wait until after dinner?"

Cole stopped chewing halfway through a bite and looked at me suspiciously, then at Shawn, and then at LuLu. She cocked her head to the side, insisting she was innocent in this ambush. Cole swallowed, wiped his mouth and then sat back in his chair, calm and attentive. "Let's talk now," he said, maturely.

I gave Shawn a smile. He raised his eyebrows, obviously impressed with Cole's decision-making. I then focused on my son while ignoring the nerves fluttering around in my stomach. "You know Shawn and I are closer than friends, right?"

"You're in love," Cole said.

"Yes, we're in love," Shawn agreed, reaching across the table and holding my hand.

"And you know lots of people who are in love, right?" I asked Cole. "Like Jaxon and Bryce?"

"Yep!" Cole nodded, following what I was saying.

"And do you remember before Lori was born, when Jaxon and Bryce told Liam they were having a—"

"Are you having a baby?" Cole exclaimed, practically flying out of his seat. I laughed and Shawn jumped in surprise, but then laughed as well.

"Well... Yes, we are," I said, beaming at Cole. Shawn squeezed my hand.

"Oh my gosh!" Cole clapped his hands and started squealing.

"So you're happy then?" Shawn asked, but it was obvious Cole was ecstatic.

"I'm gonna have a brother or sister, just like Liam! I have to tell everyone!"

I let him use my phone on speaker to call Nicole, who already knew the good news but did a great job of acting like she was hearing it for the first time from him. Then he called Liam and a few other school friends. By the time he'd done the rounds, we were exhausted, hearing the same story over and over again, and he was looking a little tired too.

"Mom will be here to pick you up soon, kiddo," I said. "How're you feeling? What questions do you have?"

"Well..." Cole said in a small voice. "If you and Shawn are having a baby, do I have to live with Mom?"

"Oh, kiddo, no way!" I said, letting go of Shawn's hand to reach across and push a strand of hair out of Cole's face. "You're not going anywhere. You're my son just as much as this new baby is going to be my son or daughter. You're not being replaced or anything. Is that what you thought?"

"No, not really, but there was a friend at school whose dad got married and had a new baby, and my friend got sent to his mom's house."

"Well, that's not going to happen. You're an important part of the family."

"Is Shawn part of our family too?" he asked.

"He is." I nodded then grinned at Shawn.

"I'm also going to be part of your pack soon," Shawn said.

I felt my stomach clench and my heart drop. I'd wanted to tell Shawn about the issues of the claiming bite later, when we were alone. Looks like that option had been taken out of my hands.

"Not soon. We're actually postponing the ceremony for now."

Suddenly, LuLu started barking and the doorbell sounded.

"That must be Nicole." I quickly stood and grabbed Cole's bag before ushering him out of the kitchen. I glanced back at Shawn. Tears were welling in his eyes. His cheeks were flushed and his bottom lip was shaking.

"I'll just... Just hang on," I said, hurrying to answer the door.

He didn't reply. He just turned his face away.

Chapter 12 - Shawn

"When were you going to tell me you *postponed* the *claiming ceremony?*" I stood up to challenge Linc as soon as he'd closed the door behind Cole. I was barely able to contain my rising anger, and my heated cheeks probably reflected that.

"I'm sorry, I know you really—"

"No, actually, apparently you *don't* know. I was so excited to be officially *yours* and to be a member of the pack. I felt so special and loved. You can't just change your mind after making me an offer like that without even asking me how I feel. Well, I'll tell you how I feel! I feel like a jilted omega left at the altar, and we haven't even set a date for the ceremony yet. If you *have* changed your mind, tell me right now. Better yet, just walk out that door. I don't need to be abandoned *again*—"

Linc put his hands on my cheeks and stopped my tirade with a passionate kiss. I immediately calmed down when all the love and devotion he had for me seeped through his lips and into my heart. When he pulled back slightly I looked up into his warm eyes, full of compassion and tenderness.

"Absolutely nothing has changed, my love. I just want to talk to Dr. Reed to make sure the claiming bite won't hurt you or the baby," he explained. "Neither Jaxon or Greer were positive nothing could happen, and I don't want to take a risk."

I took a deep breath and felt my cheeks get ever hotter, this time with embarrassment. "Oh my god, I'm sorry," I said, covering my face with my hands. "Ughhhh, I'm such a hormonal, emotional mess." I sank into a bar stool in the kitchen. "I don't want to take that risk either... Obviously."

"I knew you would understand," Linc said patiently, stroking my cheeks with his thumbs. "I only spoke to them last night, and this was the first opportunity to tell you."

I nodded, feeling such an idiot, but that fear of abandonment wasn't something that had entirely disappeared after Phillip had run off on me. "I'm sorry. Can we just watch a cheesy romantic comedy or something? I probably just need something to cry about. Maybe I'll feel better after that."

"Of course. You go snuggle up on the couch and I'll make you a cup of tea."

I gratefully took him up on his offer, as did LuLu, following close behind me as I made my way to the living room. She curled up at my feet at the end of the lounge section of my couch and rested her chin on my foot, staring at me with concern in her wide eyes.

"It's okay, LuLu," I said in reassurance. "I was just upset over nothing."

When Linc set my tea down on the coffee table before coming to join me on the couch, I scooted up so he could sit behind me and I could rest my back against his broad, firm chest. We didn't get more than a few minutes into the movie before his affectionate nuzzles and gentle massaging of my shoulders turned into nibbles on my ear lobe and kisses on my neck. When he brought his tongue into the picture, treating the side of my neck like a melting popsicle, I let out a soft, involuntary moan.

"Sorry, am I distracting you from the movie?" he whispered in my ear.

"I'm starting to think maybe it's not the movie I need to make me feel better..." I said, running my hand up his leg to rest on his thigh.

"Say no more," Linc replied, his deep voice sending a tingle down my spine. He wrapped his arms around me then carried me off to my bedroom.

After carefully laying me down on the bed, he lay next to me and slid his hands beneath my sweater as he slowly possessed my mouth. I unbuttoned his shirt and skimmed my hands over his rippling, muscled back, reveling in the feel of him beneath my palms; his strength, his gentleness. The bed creaked as he shifted his weight to crouch over me on all fours.

"Want to make this good for you," he said, his voice a low growl. He pulled my sweater up over my head then dragged off my pants and underwear. Before I knew it, he'd drawn my cock into his mouth and started stroking the length of my shaft. When he moved his mouth to my balls, sucking on each of them one at a time, I groaned.

"That feels amazing."

Linc looked up to smile at me. "Good. Because you deserve amazing," he said, but then he changed tactics and pressed his finger against the wet opening of my hole.

I groaned again, louder this time as he took the head of my dick into his mouth once more. The combination of suction on the swollen tip of my cock with the pressure of Linc's finger pressing into my ass was enough to send me reeling. I arched my back and squirmed closer to him, and he eagerly provided me with more of what I wanted, taking me deeper into his mouth and pushing his finger all the way inside me, massaging my prostate in a maddeningly slow rhythm. Then he lifted off me and sat back on his heels.

"Do you want my cock?" he asked, his lips looking deliciously wet and red. I nodded, and he grinned before opening his jeans and wiggling out of them. Once he was as naked as me, I craned my neck to kiss him again, hungrily biting his lower lip and sucking it into my mouth. He moaned and reached down to angle his cock toward my opening, gently pressing the tip against me, then pushing harder. He reached up to touch my cheek and looked into my eyes.

"I love you," he whispered, sliding his cock deep into me before pulling out halfway.

"I love you too."

Linc leaned forward, and then started moving, gently at first, like he always did, but then building up speed until the bed rocked with the force of how hard he fucked me. I grabbed my cock, which was slapping against my stomach, and started to rub at the weeping head with my thumb. My body throbbed with pleasure as Linc thrust deeper and deeper, catching my prostate with every plunge.

"Oh, I'm gonna... I'm gonna come," I cried as my balls pulled up and heat flashed over my skin. I gripped Linc's shoulders, just as spunk shot out of my dick covering my stomach. My hole pulsated wildly around Linc's cock and he moaned loudly, leaning down to kiss me as he hammered my slick hole faster than ever before. I clenched my ass, hoping to increase the intensity of his orgasm. It seemed to work as he let out a rumbling growl just before hot liquid spilled inside me.

As he came, Linc collapsed on top of me, slowing his thrusts to a few deep pushes until he let out one final groan. I wrapped my arms around him and held him close, nuzzling my face into his neck and taking in the smell of his sweat and cologne. He raised his head and kissed me again, his lips so soft they felt like butterfly wings.

"I'm crushing you," Linc said, slowly rolling off me and lying at my side before he pulled me into his arms and held me close.

I rested my head on his chest and my hand on his hip. He was still breathing heavily, and I loved that I could do that to him; turn him into an alpha full of need and want for his omega.

"Love you," I said softly.

Linc kissed the top of my head and ran his fingers through my hair.

"Love you too, Shawn. Love you so much."

***

"Alright, let's have a look at what's going on," Dr. Reed said in a confident, professional tone. It was my first appointment and I felt a flutter of nerves in my belly as I took off my shirt to start the ultrasound.

Dr. Reed squeezed warm gel onto my stomach and started moving the ultrasound wand around, looking for the fetus growing inside me. I watched her slide it left, right, up and down. Then left again. I looked at Linc. He smiled at me contentedly. Knowing he wasn't worried calmed me down a little. Still, I craned my neck to try and look at the screen of the ultrasound machine, but I couldn't see it from my position on the bed.

The wand finally came to rest. I looked at Dr. Reed's face expectantly.

"Very good, we've got a heartbeat," she said with a smile. I exhaled loudly and laughed with relief. Linc squeezed my hand and I turned to smile at him. His grin was already threatening to split his face in two.

"Wow," he said. He looked like a little kid on Christmas morning.

"Hmm, hang on," Dr. Reed said, moving the wand slightly again. My head whipped back to look at her.

"What is it?" I asked, worry slamming into me.

"I'm not sure, it might be another heartbeat."

"Oh my gosh," I whispered to Linc. "Twins?"

"I hadn't even considered twins…" Linc covered his mouth in shock.

"Nope, sorry, false alarm. Just one heartbeat, but it's *very* strong," Dr. Reed said with a smile.

Linc and I sighed in unison. "Disappointed?" I asked Linc.

"Not at all. I think I'm relieved, actually. One baby is plenty of baby for me," he added with a smile.

"Well, everything looks healthy. You're about ten weeks along, so we can see you again in a couple of more months to determine the sex, if that's what you want."

Linc nodded before looking at me. "Do you want to know the sex of our baby?" he asked, as if realizing I had a say in this too.

I smiled. "Yes, please, when we can."

Dr. Reed made a note on her chart, then glanced between Linc and me. "Is there anything else you want to ask me?"

"Um," Linc said, biting his bottom lip and looking nervous. "Yes, actually. Maybe you can help us… I spoke to Jaxon and some of the other alphas, but no one seems to have an idea what might happen if I give Shawn a claiming bite. Will that have any effect on him or the baby? We were planning a ceremony, but I wouldn't want to risk any complications for either of them."

"There shouldn't be any complications… I've never heard of any."

"But Shawn is human. That's different, right—because I'll be turning him and not just claiming him as if he were already a shifter."

"I don't see why. There have been plenty of humans turned with the claiming bite."

"Pregnant humans?"

"He's carrying a shifter baby; the bite definitely won't affect the unborn child. The only difference is that Shawn won't be able to shift until after he's given birth."

"I know that, but—"

"Linc, in all my years as a doctor, I have never heard of any complications. Jaxon claimed Bryce while he was pregnant."

"I know, but—"

"Linc, I think what Dr. Reed is saying, is that there won't be an issue," I said gently as it was obvious Linc would continue to argue. He was worried, and that was fine, but I didn't want him pissing off the doctor who was going to be my obstetrician during my pregnancy.

Dr. Reed nodded. "Exactly. The baby is in good health from what I can tell, and it's not a high-risk pregnancy."

Linc finally nodded. "Thank you, Maddie." He bit down on his bottom lip, but then looked at me. I smiled up at him, trying to be positive.

"Thank you so much, Dr. Reed," I said, clambering off the table.

"You're very welcome. Congratulations! I'm looking forward to the claiming ceremony."

"Thank you! Me too," I said, ushering Linc out of the examination room. I hoped that would be the end of Linc's worries, but as we got into the elevator, Linc shook his head.

"I think we need to get a second opinion."

"From who?" I asked. "Do you know of another wolf shifter obstetrician." I threw out the problem in an attempt for Linc to drop the matter, but Linc nodded.

"There are other packs in Timberwood Cove, and in other towns. It's Jaxon's job to keep in touch with all the pack leaders, so I'm sure he'd be able to find other doctors."

I sighed. I was perfectly content with Dr. Reed's opinion, and though I didn't want to push Linc into claiming me when it was obvious he wasn't comfortable with it, getting a second opinion seemed too much. "Linc—"

The elevator door slid open, and in order not to have a heated discussion in the middle of the hospital, I bit my lip—only to gasp when I saw who was standing at the reception desk. "Shit!"

Linc stared down at me. "I know you don't want to wait, but—"

"It's not that. It's… We have to go. Now." I grabbed Linc's hand and pulled him out the door to the parking lot, and then started speed walking to the car.

"You're gonna pull my arm out of the socket, Shawn. What's going on? Do you have a pregnancy craving or something?"

"Did you see that guy standing at the reception desk?" I asked, unable to keep my voice from sounding high and sharp.

"No? Why?"

"Do you think he saw me? Shit, what if he saw me?"

"I have no idea. Shawn… What. Is. Going. On?" Linc growled.

When we reached the car I leaned my back against the passenger side door and tried to catch my breath. I felt dizzy, feverish, and the world seemed to be spinning around me.

"Shawn? Are you okay?" Linc's words floated into my mind as if he were walking toward me through a thick fog.

"That was Phillip," I said, my voice now flat as a sort of numbness invaded my body.

"Your *ex* Phillip?"

I nodded, folding my arms against my chest as an attempt to steady myself.

"So? He's out of your life now. You don't have to worry about him."

I blinked, trying to accept what Linc was saying. He was right, Phillip was out of my life, but seeing him...

Linc pulled my arms free and held my hands. "Want me to go back in there and beat him up? He's already in the hospital..."

I laughed, and the jolt of the laughter shook me out of the numbing fog. But I still felt a lump sitting uneasily in my throat. "Let's just go," I managed to say. Linc opened the door for me and I slid into the passenger seat.

"Are you sure you're alright?" Linc asked after a few minutes of silence on the way home.

"I'm a little shaken up, to be honest," I said. "Seeing Phillip reminded me how it felt to be drop-kicked out of his life. Ever since then I've been afraid of it happening again. Sometimes I'm so afraid it gets to a point of being irrational..." I looked over at Linc to see if he caught the reference to my hysterics the other day after I found out he wanted to delay the claiming ceremony.

"Mm..." Linc said diplomatically.

"It's just that *now* I have to think of the *baby* too," I said, feeling despondent again. "What would we do if you left us? It'd just be me and the little one against the world."

Linc glanced at me and reached out to squeeze my knee. "I'm not going to abandon you. You're my fated mate. Shifters *never* abandon their mate. You're everything I've wanted. Everything I've been searching for. Nothing is going to pry me away from you. Besides, Phillip was a jerk. He probably still is."

I sighed and placed my hand over Linc's. I leaned my head back against the seat and closed my eyes. I felt so lucky to have met someone capable of fully committing to me. I took another deep breath to shake off my residual panic. "Thanks for saying that, Linc. I know you've said it so many times before, but...it helps."

"Anytime, my love. I'll say it as many times as you need me to." Linc flashed me another smile. "I love you, Shawn. We're meant to be together, and I am going to make sure we get to stay together, whatever happens."

When we got back to Linc's house, I decided to take a nap. I got out some comfortable pajamas from the drawer Linc had cleared out for me and took off my shirt. Linc walked into the room but stopped just a few steps from the doorway.

"Oh my god, Shawn!"

"What?" I turned around to see if he was gasping at something on the wall behind me. I didn't see anything unusual. "What is it?"

"Your baby bump is showing," Linc said, sounding giddy.

"Really?" I looked down at my belly. It seemed the same as it normally did from that angle.

"Yes. Come here, look in the mirror."

Linc grabbed my hand and pulled me over to the full-length mirror. He rotated me to the side so he could show me a profile view of my torso. "See?" He pointed just above the waist band of my pants.

I cocked my head to the side and squinted, and my heart started racing when I realized he was right. There was a slightly curved bulge happening. "Oh my god, you're right."

"I know! And it looks...*so good* on you," Linc said, his voice suddenly growly and husky.

"You're really into me being pregnant, huh?" I grinned.

Linc nodded and bit his lower lip. He slid his hands over my slight bump, caressing the soft skin. Then he slid them around to my ass and pulled me gently against him. His thickening cock immediately made my cock stand to attention too.

I inhaled sharply, intensely aroused by just standing here, being held by my alpha. Linc slid his hands off my ass and took a step back before grasping my fingers and pulling me with him toward the bed. We tumbled into the mattress, and I eagerly stripped out of my pants and underwear, watching as Linc did the same. I slid one of my legs between his as we lay facing each other. Linc kissed me, his lips sweetly addictive. I pressed closer to him, parting my lips to taste him better, moaning before sliding my tongue inside his mouth.

My cock was wedged against Linc's meaty thigh, and I gave in to my urge to rub it against him. I started leaking precum making the glide easier, but I wanted more. I slid my hand down Linc's torso to reach for his heavy cock. He followed suit, grasping my cock and starting to stroke it. I groaned as a sizzle of desire seared my nerves. I loved it when Linc touched me, when he looked after me like this. He wasn't like other alphas who demanded to be pleasured without caring about their omega's gratification. Linc was always so considerate and attentive. It's what made him so special.

We started up a rhythm of soft squeezes and slick strokes, until I was so close I could barely keep my hand moving, so lost in the need to come nothing else seemed to matter. Linc must have known because he gripped both our cocks in his big hand and increased speed. I cried out just as Linc grunted, and then I felt a warm splash against my stomach, realizing a split second before pleasure blasted through me that Linc had come all over me. Gasping, I shuddered and shivered through my release, whimpering as Linc continued to stroke me until he'd squeezed every last drop of cum out of my cock.

Afterward, when my senses returned, Linc reached for a tissue to wipe us off, and then I snuggled into his arms for a deep, blissful nap.

Chapter 13 - Linc

Early June, and the cottonwoods were flowering, spring birds were chirping, and Shawn's tiny baby bump had turned into a full-on basketball belly. I glanced up from the kitchen bench to see his silhouette lit by lamplight as he leaned over Cole's desk in the living room, helping him with his homework.

"Twenty-two times three…" Cole was mumbling, then quickly jotting down the answer.

"Great job," Shawn said, encouraging him. "What about this one? Looks tricky."

"No way, it's easy!" Cole insisted.

Shawn laughed, and rubbed the top of Cole's head. Cole grinned, and I realized how much they'd gotten close over the last few months. Cole truly adored Shawn, and I knew Shawn loved Cole. Shawn was good with kids, and there was no doubt he'd be a good father.

Once I had the roast vegetables in the oven, I looked up again and saw Cole was working on his own with LuLu asleep at his feet. Shawn was on the other side of the room, sitting on the couch with a stack of medical books beside him and one open in his lap. I wiped my hands on a dish towel as I hurried over to stand behind him. I put a hand on his shoulder as I leaned over and kissed his cheek before gazing down at the research he was doing.

"That looks, uh… Gross?"

A full-page illustration showed a comparison of the internal organs in wolves and humans in way too much detail for me to stomach.

"Just trying to learn everything I can about the bite. The medical books I got from Jaxon were helpful to a degree, but they didn't actually mention the claiming ceremony. Greer lent me this one…" He picked up a book from the pile. "But it's written in a way that the existence of shifters, and the bite to convert humans into shifters is nothing more than folklore," he mumbled.

"That's probably because if a human got hold of that book or others like it, then it would seem more like fiction than reality. We've had to keep it that way."

"Yeah, but it doesn't help me now."

I squeezed his shoulder then came around to sit beside him. I couldn't help but gaze at his beautiful belly. I loved the way it pushed out his shirt. He'd put on a little baby weight, and it seriously turned me on by how his hips had filled out.

"I'm sorry we've had to wait for the ceremony," I said softly, dragging my eyes up to look at his face.

Shawn sighed and looked at me with pleading eyes. "We haven't spoken about it for a while… Can we? Dr. Reed said it was safe…"

"We don't know for certain though. You've done research, and there isn't anything to indicate it's safe for you." My heart started racing at the thought of hurting my mate and unborn baby with my bite.

"There's nothing to say it's not safe either," Shawn insisted.

"Are you talking about the baby?" Cole asked as he spun around in his chair.

Shawn glanced at me to say this discussion wasn't over, and then he turned to face Cole. "Yeah, buddy we are," Shawn replied, and patted the seat beside him. "You know what? We're going to see if it's a boy or a girl tomorrow."

Cole hurried over and LuLu lifted her head for a moment before resting it back down with a sigh. She'd calmed down now that Shawn was really showing. I wondered if she'd just been anxious about the change in his body and had now gotten used to it.

"I think you should call it Errol," Cole said as he sat on the other side of Shawn.

"Errol?" I asked.

"Errrrol!" Cole said, rolling his r's for as long as he could manage.

"We'll take it under advisement," I said.

"What if the baby is a girl?" Shawn asked.

"It won't be a girl." Cole scrunched up his nose.

"Uh, it might be," I warned him. "What would be so bad about that? Liam has a little sister, and that's cool, right?"

"Yeah, so we have one little sister in our pack, and now we need a little brother," he explained to me in a tone that suggested he thought I was an idiot.

Shawn laughed and nodded. "Duh, Dad."

"Yeah, duh, Dad."

"That's enough out of you two," I growled. "Seriously, what girl names do we have?"

"Nicole!" Cole exclaimed and I raised my eyebrows.

"Sure, maybe," I said, then gave Shawn a look that said "awkward".

"Any other ideas, buddy?" he asked Cole.

"Hm, I don't know any other girl names," he said with a shrug.

Over dinner, we ran through the names of all the women in his life to remind him that he knew plenty of girl names, and Cole scrunched up his nose at every one, though he conceded that "Sam" would be nice for either a girl or a boy. Shawn said that "Kyle" or "Kylie" were his favorites. I agreed with both of them.

Once dinner was done and Cole was asleep in bed with LuLu, Shawn and I hurried to the bedroom and closed the door. My breath hitched as I watched him shake off his shirt in the moonlight that spilled in through the window. I sat on the edge of the bed and watched attentively as he took off his pants while he looked at me with a sweet grin. My gaze flicked from his face down to his bulging belly, the tightness of his briefs over his crotch, and then back up to his eyes. He gave me a cheeky grin and stepped closer.

"Your turn," he said, tugging at the hem of my sweater. I obediently lifted my arms, and he got me topless before running his cool hands over my shoulders, his long fingers pressing into the muscles there and sending a warm wave of relaxation through my body. I let out an appreciative sigh, closing my eyes for a moment before pulling him closer to me.

Shawn straddled my lap with a knee either side of my hips, and I reached down to hold his ass with both of my hands. He moaned and pressed his lips against mine in a soft, sweet kiss. I squeezed his ass and smiled into his kiss as he let out a short moan. He pushed me down onto the bed, and Shawn grazed his hand over my chest hair, tickling his fingers through it as he smiled at me. I ran a hand over his belly. A deep breath pushed into my lungs as a rush of excitement shivered down my spine. Shawn let out a groan and snuggled closer to me.

"I love you so much," he whispered, planting soft kisses on my neck. I moaned from the tingle his lips evoked and wrapped my arms around him, bringing him closer to me.

"I love you, Shawn." I sighed happily. "I've never felt this way before about anybody."

He kissed me again, but then pulled away and sighed. "I want you to claim me so badly," he groaned.

"I know." I kissed the spot where I would place the bite. "I will."

"Promise?" he asked.

"Yes, my love," I said, tracing my finger over his neck. "I promise." My heart ached with not being able to give Shawn what he wanted right now. I wanted to make Shawn happy, but I still felt like I couldn't risk it. I'd waited so long for a mate, for Shawn. I just couldn't take the chance something would go wrong. As soon as he gave birth, however, I intended to claim him and make him mine forever.

I reached down and touched Shawn's belly again. He moved so he was lying on his back, and we both gazed at his protruding bump. I spread my fingers wide so I could hold his belly with as much of my hand as I could.

"Hey little babe," I said, as I moved my hand in circles. "We can't wait to meet you."

"And we just cannot wait to find out if you're a boy or a girl," Shawn added.

"Oh yeah." I smiled up at Shawn then turned back to talk to his tummy. "We're going to see a picture of you tomorrow. Wave for us, alright?"

I gasped and Shawn almost jumped out of his skin.

"What is it?"

"It moved. Look!" I took my hand away and revealed a lump protruding out of his belly, wriggling around and then disappearing. Shawn gasped and we stared at his belly, now still. In slow motion, we looked up and stared at each other, wide-eyed, mouths open, and completely amazed.

"Oh my god," he said, and then burst out laughing. "I thought that feeling in my tummy was just gas!"

***

The stenographer's office was stark white, smelled like alcohol swabs, and was downright scary. Luckily, it was located on the far side of the hospital and Shawn got us in via a staff door so we didn't have to spend too much time in the stink of the main building. My stomach was still churning a little from the sterile smell of the office, but Cole didn't seem to care—he was happily sitting by a desk, swinging his legs and staring at the anatomical posters on the wall. Shawn certainly didn't have the heightened senses to care about the smell, and I almost said he should be happy he wasn't a shifter yet... But I wisely bit my tongue. I sat beside him and held his hand as he lay on the table waiting for the stenographer.

"Alright then, Mr. Drocella," the young stenographer said as she came in the room, and then she quickly looked up from the chart she was staring at. "Oh! Shawn! Hi!"

"Hi there, Alice." Shawn smiled warmly. "This is Linc, and his son Cole."

"Pleasure to meet you." Alice shook my hand. "Shawn is everyone's favorite nurse to deal with on the rounds, so I'm honored to have him in my office today."

Shawn laughed and swatted at her to make her stop, but I could tell he was actually flattered.

"And you, Cole, do you like lollipops?" she asked.

"Hm, sometimes." he said, swinging his legs.

"Well, if you want to look in that drawer there, you can take as many as you want."

"Actually, he can have one," I said, glaring at Cole to dare him to argue.

Cole jumped down to rifle through the drawer Alice had pointed out, triumphantly pulling out what must have been the largest in there. I shook my head, but I wasn't about to take it off him. Hopefully he'd have enough sense not to try and eat it all at the same time.

"Okay, let's spread this goop," Alice said as she held up a bottle of lubricant and motioned for Shawn to lift up his top.

"Oh my gosh, it's so cold," he hissed as she smeared it on. "I thought patients were just too sensitive and whiny when they complained about this, but it really is cold. Every time it happens, I'm *still* shocked!"

Alice chuckled, pulled up a stool next to the stenography machine, and then grabbed the wand. "I'm going to push kind of hard so that we can get a good look, but let me know if you want me to stop or pull back, okay?"

Shawn nodded, and I grabbed his hand. He looked at me and gave me an excited grin. My heart was racing and my leg started bouncing. Alice moved the wand around Shawn's belly for ages, and I kept my eyes on his face to make sure he was comfortable and not putting himself in any serious discomfort. He was staring at the screen for most of the time, but kept glancing back at me to give me excited smiles.

"Okay, here's a good angle," Alice said, pressing a button that locked the screen. "Oh!" She quickly covered the screen with a hand. "Do you want to know the sex?"

"Yes!" Shawn said as I nodded.

"Cole, want to see?" I gestured for him to come closer.

"Is it a brother or a sister?" he asked with a lollipop stick hanging out of his mouth.

"It is..." Alice said, peeling her hand away. "A brother!"

"Yes!" Cole exclaimed before pumping the air with his fist and dancing around the room. I leaned down and kissed Shawn's cheek as he stared at the monitor.

"He's beautiful," he sighed. I looked up and suddenly felt my wolf's protective instincts more intensely than ever before. The silhouette of our son was wriggling around on the screen, and I could see his tiny nose was the same angle as Shawn's.

"He looks so much like you," I said.

"His arms look so strong, like yours," he said, beaming up at me.

"He looks very strong... Very large for this far along. But hey, he seems healthy to me," Alice said, pressing buttons to take snapshots of the ultrasound. "I'll send these images to your obstetrician. Who is..." She glanced at her chart and frowned.

"Dr. Maddie Reed," I interjected.

"Reed? Alright," she said, making a note on her chart. "I'll get these to her this afternoon, and I'm sure she'll call you about scheduling an appointment if there are any results she wants to discuss."

"Thanks, Alice," Shawn said, reaching out and taking her hand.

"You're so welcome. And congratulations, both of you. Can't wait to meet this little guy!"

"Neither can we." I smiled at Shawn again, unable to hide how thrilled I was we were having a healthy baby.

For the rest of the day, I couldn't keep my hands off Shawn's belly. Driving home, I reached over and rested one hand against his bulge. At home, I kept coming up behind him and rubbing his tummy with my fingertips. By the time we went to bed that night, I was practically drooling as Shawn took off his shirt. I grabbed him before he could put on his pajamas, and we fell into bed, kissing. This time, the sweetness of last night's cuddle was replaced with pure lust. Shawn hungrily slid his tongue into my mouth. I growled and greedily grabbed at anything I could reach—his shoulders, his ass, his belly and finally his cock. I moaned as I found him already hard.

Suddenly, he pulled back and crinkled his nose.

"What's wrong?" I asked, quickly pulling my hands away.

"Heartburn," he grumbled, sitting up in bed and placing a hand on his chest. "Oh god, it's a bad one."

I let out a sigh of relief when I realized it wasn't anything more severe, but then Shawn pushed me away and made a foul face.

"It's really bad."

"I'll get you some ginger ale." I raced downstairs to the kitchen. When I came back to the bedroom with the usual home remedies of ginger ale and plain crackers, Shawn still looked like he was in pain. "Is it... Should we call Maddie?" I asked, my wolf pushing me into protective mode.

"No, no, it's fine. It's been worse. Just, wow, bad timing."

He sipped his ginger ale, and I sat beside him. When he'd finished, I wrapped my arm around his shoulders and pulled him close. He let out a sigh and lay his head on my chest. We stayed entwined together like that until his heartburn subsided, and then we scooted down under the covers, and I spooned Shawn from behind, loving the feeling of him in my arms.

"Remember when we lay on the beach and wished on a falling star?" Shawn asked me with a wistful sigh. "Well, all of my wishes have come true," he said with a sparkle in his voice.

"And what wishes were those?" I asked.

"I wished I could have a baby of my own, even though I fully believed that would never happen, and I also wished you would never leave me, which you've promised not to do," he said as he wriggled his butt against me.

"Funny," I said, reminiscing on that night on the beach. "I wished for the same things. I mean, I knew I never wanted to leave you. But I also wished we could have a baby," I said. Then I sleepily kissed his forehead just before I started drifting off.

Chapter 14 - Shawn

I should have been happy about what Linc said. But I wasn't. I felt like a boulder was suddenly crushing my heart, and it wasn't from heartburn. I thought Linc loved me for who I was. I confessed my believed infertility to him early on because I didn't want our relationship to have any false pretenses. And he told me it was fine with him, that he didn't need any more kids. Now he'd completely contradicted his assurances. I felt sick. My stomach churned, and breathing felt like bench pressing a huge barbell.

Am I overreacting? I knew my hormonal mood swings didn't help me emotionally, but I felt too deeply hurt for this to just be a mood. Linc made me believe he loved me exactly as I was, and that *clearly* wasn't true. He must have been secretly wishing I could be different, that I would be something *more*, something closer to an ideal partner who could give him children. He must have been if he was secretly wishing I would get pregnant.

What a jerk!

While I was running through the situation in my mind, Linc was drifting off to sleep, and by the time I had come to the conclusion that he didn't love me the way he said he did, I heard him snoring. The fact that he could fall asleep right after revealing his dishonesty to me was appalling. It was too much for me to handle. Tears started to fall onto my pillow. I sniffed and wiped my nose, curling up on my side to try and comfort myself enough to get some sleep. It was time, I decided, to just accept what I had suspected all along: no one could love me just the way I was. No matter how open and trusting I tried to be.

***

The next morning, I got ready for work as usual. Linc had gotten up first and was already downstairs making breakfast, so I took my time getting dressed while I silently nursed my broken heart. By the time I made my way down to the kitchen, Linc and Cole had finished eating. LuLu trotted over to me immediately and jumped up on my leg.

"Hello, sweet puppy." I tried to keep my tone as loving as always, but she looked at me with worried eyes. She always knew when I was suffering.

"Want some oats, my love?" Linc asked.

"I'm not hungry," I said flatly. I wasn't ready to tell him how hurt I was, and I didn't have it in me to pretend like everything was okay either.

"Morning sickness?" Linc asked as he poured coffee into a travel mug.

I ignored his question and went to get my coat and bag ready.

"Are you nauseous this morning, Shawn?" Cole asked.

"Yeah, a little," I said, somewhat honestly since my stricken heart was making me feel ill.

"That sucks," Cole said.

"That *stinks*," Linc said, correcting him.

"I can't say *sucks*?"

"Do your teachers at school let you say 'suck' in class?" Linc asked.

"No," Cole grumbled quietly, pushing around the last of his porridge with his spoon.

"Exactly. Are you done eating?" Linc replied.

Cole nodded and dropped his spoon in his bowl. He got up and came over to me and hugged my side tightly as I was putting my coat on.

"Have you felt my little brother move today?" he asked me.

"No, not yet," I answered softly, perfectly happy to talk to Cole even if I wasn't talking to his father.

"Can I feel?" he asked me hopefully. LuLu trotted over to watch.

"Sure can," I said, holding my coat open so he could put his little hands on my belly over my shirt. He placed his palms gently on either side of my belly, then started humming a tune.

"My little baby *brotherrr*," he sang. "Can you hear me? Tap once if you can *hearrrrr* me." He waited in silence for a moment to see if the baby would offer a reply. "Errol?" Cole asked, turning his head to the side as if he would be able to hear the baby inside my belly. Then suddenly, I felt a squirm. Then a wriggle. Then a hard kick! I laughed and Cole's face lit up with delight.

"I guess that's your answer," I said to Cole with a smile. "I think he might be excited to meet you."

"I love you!" Cole shouted at my stomach.

LuLu barked, panting happily as she looked from Cole to me and then back again.

"I'm sure the little guy loves you already," I said. "I'm going to zip up my coat now, though. We don't want to be late."

"Yeah, I *guesssss*," Cole said with more than a hint of disappointment.

Linc came over and handed me the travel mug with coffee. I took it wordlessly, and he bent down to lace up his boots.

"Alright, we ready?" he asked with a smile when his boots were done up. He didn't have a clue how much pain I was in. My heart sank yet again knowing he hadn't noticed I was ignoring him. Cole and I nodded in answer to his question and we headed to the car with LuLu right behind us.

After dropping off Cole and LuLu at their respective schools, Linc turned the car toward the hospital.

"What the hell is eating *you* this morning?" he asked suddenly as we stopped at a red light.

I looked at him coldly, and then turned to gaze out the window stoically. I let a few moments pass to let him know that he wasn't convincing me of his love and concern with his aggressive question.

"Shawn?"

I sighed loudly and crossed my arms.

"What is it? Is it something I said?" he asked. He thought for a moment. "Did I put too much milk in your coffee again?"

"The coffee's fine," I said quietly even though I hadn't tasted it.

"Then *what*?" Linc lifted his hands off the steering wheel in a gesture of frustration. The light changed to green and he looked back to the road.

"Last night…" I took a deep breath to steady myself before launching into my explanation. "You told me you'd wished for a baby—on the falling star we saw that night on the beach. But every time we discussed children, family, and my infertility before that, you said it wasn't a problem. That we were fated mates and it didn't matter, and you didn't need to have more children, and you loved me exactly as I was. That I was everything you wanted and more, but—" My voice cracked and I took a moment to sniff back tears. Linc remained dead silent. "But… If you wished for me to have a baby even though you knew I was *sterile*, then I guess I wasn't so perfect for you, was I? I guess there was more that you wanted. And I just didn't measure up. And as far as you knew, I never *would* measure up."

I was getting angry now, firing words at him like projectiles. He kept driving to the hospital and didn't make an effort to deny what I was saying. Tears welled in my eyes but that didn't stop me from telling him exactly how I felt.

"Not to mention you *keep* postponing the goddamn claiming ceremony! So I know you *say* you'll never leave me, and you'll always care for me, and that all sounds very nice. But do your actions really measure up, Linc? Do they line up with the promises you love to make?"

Linc pulled into the hospital parking lot, and then turned to me as he pulled the handbrake on. He opened his mouth, but I shook my head, stopping him from interrupting my tirade. Linc damn well needed to listen to me.

"I don't know if I can keep pretending everything is fine and we have a perfect, fated relationship when apparently you don't actually mean half the things you say to me. I don't know if I can keep going on like this! I'm ready to throw in the towel. I'd rather be a single father than constantly feel like my heart is going to be broken. I can't *live* like this, not knowing where you stand!"

Chapter 15 - Linc

"Wh—what?" I stuttered. "Shawn, you know where I stand with *everything*. You're my mate. You're carrying my child."

Shawn crossed his arms over his chest and glared at me. My heart began to pound as panic set in. What the hell could I say to prove something that was so obvious to me? My wolf was grumbling, my mind was spinning, and I felt like my throat was stuffed full of cotton wool. Even if I could find the right thing to say, I wasn't sure I could get the words out without fumbling over them.

I turned back to the wheel and gazed out of the windscreen as I took a deep breath and collected myself. I realized I was talking to someone whose pregnancy hormones were in overdrive, and I needed to speak to him with some semblance of calm and a whole lot of sensitivity.

"Listen," I said in a low tone. "I would love you even if we had never become pregnant. I would love you no matter what, and I already knew that. I made the wish because I had a feeling that was what *you* were wishing for. You wanted to have kids, right?"

I swallowed nervously before I glanced at him. His eyes seemed to soften for a moment, and I felt my shoulders relaxing. I unclenched my fingers from around the wheel and was about to reach for his hand when his face hardened again, he inhaled sharply and threw open the truck door.

"Shawn!" I cried, but he was already out, slamming the door behind him before sashaying across the parking lot toward the hospital.

"Fuck!" My wolf howled and snarled, clawing at my chest, and a brutal anger erupted from my soul. "Fuck, fuck, fuck!"

My tires screeched as I pulled out of the parking lot and flew up Pack Lane, heading straight home. Blood was still racing through me, and I felt hot as hell as I pulled up to the house.

I immediately sent Shawn a text. *Are we okay??*

It took him all of two minutes to reply. *Not even close. Don't talk to me!!!!!!*

My hands were shaking and my legs felt like jelly as I stalked across the yard, heading straight for the woods. I thought a gentle walk would help calm me down, but every step seemed to make me more furious. My mind reeled with frustration, my chest was tight, and my jaw was clenched hard enough to break my teeth. And under it all, my wolf was starting to feel trapped and constricted, and I knew how he felt.

I needed to free both of us.

As soon as my boots hit the edge of the forest, I shifted, sprinting into the woods in an effort to release some tension. As I ran, I tried to push aside the pain Shawn's words evoked. His lack of trust in me hurt, but the fact he was also in pain kept haunting my wolf, and as we came to a clearing he threw back his head and howled in mourning for the loss of his mate. Suddenly, I heard an answering howl coming from the direction of the homestead. I stiffened, waiting to hear if it a warning or an alarm. A crash through the underbrush made my fur stand on end. And then I smelled Jaxon and Gavin on the wind and realized they had heard me and were racing to my aid. I growled and looked around for an escape. The last thing I wanted to do was share my grief. I ran off deeper into the woods, determined to be alone.

Unfortunately, I'd already burned through most of my energy, and the other wolves quickly caught up to me. I sprinted down well-worn tracks in the hopes of out-running them, but they nipped at my heels. My lungs burned. My muscles felt weak and numb, and as the path turned sharply to the left, my paws gave out and I skidded to the right. I fell onto my side and slid for a moment before I thumped heavily against a moss-covered tree trunk. Spring growth floated down like green rain all around me. I lay there, panting and staring out at the path as eight long legs came into view.

Jaxon nudged my belly with his snout as though urging me to get up. I covered my face with my paw and grumbled. Gavin growled and nipped at my haunches and I immediately shot up onto four paws from the shock of it. I growled at him. He snarled back at me and pawed at the ground in warning. I lowered my head and bared my teeth. Most of me didn't want to fight him, but if he pushed it, I'd take him down. Just as Gavin was lowering his head and peeling his lips back aggressively, Jaxon lunged and nipped at my neck. I spun around and he leaped back, then lunged again and nipped me harder. I yelped, and before I had the chance to respond, he shifted into his human form.

I reluctantly followed the lead of my pack alpha and shifted. Gavin followed close behind. I sat on my ass in the forest, resting my back against the tree I'd hit, panting hard as I looked up at the canopy.

"Fuck," I groaned.

"What the hell is going on?" Gavin demanded as he stood with his hands on his hips. "I was in the middle of important work when I heard you yapping away in the forest and had to come after you."

"I didn't ask you to. I was just blowing off some steam."

Jaxon cleared his throat and crouched down in front of me. "What's going on?"

"Nothing," I snapped, then clenched my jaw. He waited, and it didn't take long before my defenses softened. "Had a fight with Shawn."

"Well, obviously." Gavin rolled his eyes, and then knelt down next to Jaxon and looked at me seriously. "What's going on?"

"He thinks I need him to be someone he's not."

"Do you?" Gavin asked.

"No! God, that's what I'm saying!" I groaned and covered my face with my hands. "But how the hell am I supposed to talk about my feelings if all he does is misunderstand me? I feel like it doesn't matter what I say—he's made up his mind that I'm a jerk and that I don't want to be with him."

Jaxon let out an understanding hum, and Gavin sighed.

"Did he break up with you?" he asked.

"I don't know," I said honestly. "He told me not to talk to him."

"Give him some time," Gavin said, putting a hand on my knee in support.

"You're fated. It will work out," Jaxon said.

"Not all fated mates ends up together," I grumbled.

Gavin nodded. "But most of the time they do. You have to work on it, and you have to trust that it'll work out. I'd *kill* to have your opportunity, Linc. Don't blow it."

I took a deep breath and sighed. "Maybe you're right."

"Just give him time."

"Gavin," Jaxon said, motioning to the trail. "Keep tabs on Shawn. Make sure he's safe while all of this is going on. And the baby."

"And LuLu," I added.

Gavin nodded, shifted, and sprinted off down the trail while Jaxon moved closer to me.

"I feel like this is bad karma for breaking up with Nicole," I said. Jaxon looked at me with wide eyes and then let out a sharp laugh. I jumped and then glared at him. "What?"

"Karma, huh? You find your fated mate and you think it's some kind of punishment? Get over yourself, Linc. You and Nicole weren't right for each other, and you both knew that."

I couldn't argue his point, but that still didn't change the fact that I'd loved her and yet I still left her. Was Shawn right after all; that I said I loved someone only to leave them when things didn't turn out the way I wanted? But I *was* getting what I wanted with Shawn—I was getting *him*.

"You'll get him back," Jaxon said as he stood and brushed off his pants.

I stood also, but I didn't have the same confidence Jaxon did. Jaxon hadn't seen the look of devastation on Shawn's face.

Chapter 16 - Shawn

My heart shattered the moment I slammed Linc's truck door behind me. At first I thought it was from the anger that bubbled inside me—all I could think about was how dare he postpone the ceremony without talking to me about it. But my anger burned out as I stormed across the parking lot, and it was barely an ember by the time I made it inside the hospital. All that was left was an ache in my chest, and a serious desire to sob my heart out.

I did my best to make it through my shift without crying, and failed. I cried when my supervisor said good morning to me, and I cried when the snack machine wouldn't accept my dollar bills. I had to excuse myself from the break room to sob outside, and I constantly sniffled as I made my way through my rounds.

"You okay, Shawn?" one of my favorite patients asked me as I checked on her in the morning. She was the mother of the young girl I'd met in the dog park months ago, with the black poodle who loved LuLu. She'd just had another baby, this one just as cute as her daughter.

"Me?" I asked, my voice wobbling as I put a hand on my chest. "I'm just...fine!"

She clucked her tongue and looked at me with sympathy. "You don't have to tell me what's going on, but it's plain as day you need to talk to someone. Or just get all those emotions out. It's not right to hold all that pain inside," she said, placing her hand on mine. I immediately got choked up and had to excuse myself. Then I rushed to the bathroom and bawled my eyes out.

But she was right. I felt a little better after letting it out. By the time my shift was over, I was feeling somewhat put together—until I remembered that Linc had driven me to work and I had no way of getting home or picking up LuLu from Trevor's. I stood at the doors of the hospital and looked out at the trees moving in the wind, and the light dwindling as the sun set.

Well, it's not going to get any warmer. I threw my scarf around my neck and started walking down the street. I got as far as the intersection of Poplar Road and Pack Lane when I just could not catch my breath. I stopped outside the video game store on the corner and sat on a bench the store had painted with some wild looking cartoon characters. One of them was a werewolf with a mean look on its face and fangs dripping with blood. I felt tears welling up in my eyes before I burst out laughing. I could not believe my life! If someone had told me five months ago I'd be pregnant, I wouldn't have believed them. And if they'd told me the father would be a wolf shifter, who was part of a pack that lived in Timberwood Cove? Outrageous! I couldn't stop laughing, and soon my sides were aching from it.

I was breathing through my laughter and trying to get myself to stop giggling when I heard a car pull up behind me. I turned to see who it was, and then burst into another fit of giggles when I saw it was a member of the pack.

"Hey, Shawn," Gavin said with a smile. "You need a lift somewhere?"

His question sobered me up. Had Linc sent him to look after me? I almost refused Gavin's offer on that basis, but I was tired, and it was getting late. Reluctantly, I nodded.

Gavin turned off the car then jumped out to help me even though I didn't need any help, but maybe they were Linc's orders. Could Linc order another alpha who had equal standing in the pack? Maybe Gavin was doing this simply because he was a nice guy.

"You work at this store, right?" I pointed to the video game store. "I've sometimes seen you in there on my way home from work."

"Well, not really... I invent and code games, and they sell them, so I'm in there a lot, but I don't actually work there."

I nodded. That kind of made sense. It would also explain why he was in the vicinity. Gavin insisted on helping me into the truck, and his consideration made it easy for me to let him. I had to admit, it felt good to have such a protective man around me after such a vulnerable day at work. It also made me miss Linc even more, but I tried to push the thought from my mind.

I sighed as Gavin buckled my seatbelt for me. Linc used to do that. He said he wanted to make sure I was always safe.

"Are you alright, Shawn?"

"No," I managed to say through the sudden ache in my chest. "My life is a mess."

"It looks pretty good from where I'm sitting," Gavin said. "You've found your fated mate, you've got a baby on the way..."

"Trust me, it's not all that pretty."

When Gavin frowned I realized who I was talking to. Obviously Gavin would take up for his packmate.

"Speaking of babies, I need to pick up LuLu. Would you mind?"

"Not at all," Gavin said, shooting me a warm smile and putting the truck into gear.

He drove me to Trevor's, and then waited outside while I dashed in—as fast as my growing belly would allow me.

"Everything okay with you, Shawn?" Trevor asked as he eyed me up and down and held LuLu's leash out for me.

"Mm, just fine," I said as I took LuLu's leash. It was a lie, just like my others, but I was beyond trying to explain to everyone who asked. I smiled down at LuLu, who was giving me the sweetest eyes.

"And who's that out there?" Trevor peered over my shoulder at Gavin's truck.

"Just a friend of Linc's," I said, bending down to give LuLu a pat. She sniffed my hand with concern, and then licked it ravenously.

"Hm..." Trevor raised his chin. "Handsome, isn't he?"

I stood back up and glanced back to look at Gavin. For the first time I realized he was very good looking, in a playboy sort of way. He was talking to someone on his phone, and the angle of his jaw really stood out.

"Not my type, but I can put in a good word for you if you like," I said with a wink.

"Please," Trevor slapped my arm. "I don't have time for romance, not with all of these puppies who need me."

"Alright, your loss," I said, wondering if it would actually *be* a loss considering Gavin was a wolf shifter. Trevor may have thought the idea of being with a shifter kind of sexy—but being a human mate of one was not particularly easy. They had a profound sense of possessiveness, which could be kind of intimidating when focused on someone who had no idea about their dynamics. To be truthful though, when I found out about Linc I'd been tempted to say something to Trevor, but I'd promised Linc not to mention anything about the Timberwood Cove pack. Now I wondered if Trevor actually *knew* about shifters when we'd had that conversation months ago, and had tried to tell me without actually telling me. Wow. Maybe I should have listened to him and I wouldn't be in this situation now. But no. No matter if I knew about shifters or not, I still would have fallen for Linc.

"Thanks, Trevor. See you tomorrow," I said, deciding I needed to get out of there before I *did* say something to Trevor about the pack.

I hauled myself up into the cab and sat with LuLu on my lap. I would have preferred to have her put into a harness in the back seat, but Gavin didn't have a dog, and therefore didn't have a safety clip to attach LuLu to.

"Everything alright?" Gavin asked. He was off his phone now and his attention was on me.

I nodded. "Who was on the phone?" I asked, though I suspected the answer.

"Uh, just Linc, actually," he said, clearing his throat and looking out the window.

I sighed, and then looked down at LuLu who was resting her head sleepily on my knees. "How…is he?" I was barely able to squeeze out the words.

"Worried about you."

I scoffed and rolled my eyes, but I had to admit that was exactly what I was hoping he would say.

"He is. He's very protective over you," Gavin insisted.

"Yeah, which is why he wished on a star that I'd be someone different… And it's why he keeps postponing the claiming ceremony," I grumbled, crossing my arms over my chest.

Gavin looked at me and raised his eyebrows. "Do you know why he did that?"

"Because he's having second thoughts about us," I said, my voice breaking as my throat tightened. "He already has Cole, he doesn't want another baby."

Gavin's eyes looked like they were about to pop out of his head. "Wow, wrong!"

I scowled and pressed my lips together, not really wanting to get into a debate.

"Shawn, listen to me. Linc is crazy about you. He's so cut up over this, he's really devastated and worried you've broken it off with him. Maybe you can't understand how strongly he feels because you're not a wolf shifter—" I glared at him, and he quickly added, "Yet. But you're his fated mate. He's in love with you."

"Then why would he—" I swallowed, trying to get past the lump in my throat, but I couldn't, and I started to cry.

"He says stupid things. He's an alpha. We're idiots. And the ceremony… Well, you know he's worried that the claiming bite could hurt you and the baby," Gavin said softly.

I looked at him through blurry tear-filled eyes and let out a pathetic sob as something in my chest twisted painfully. "Why doesn't he trust the doctor who said it'll be okay?"

"I don't know." Gavin sighed and reached over to rub my shoulders. The touch was comforting, and I sniffled my way out of my heavy sobs. He grabbed a box of tissues from the glove compartment, and I gratefully used half the pack to blow my nose and wipe up my tears.

LuLu pawed at me and leaned up to try and lick the rest of the tears from my face.

"I'm so sorry, Gavin. I wish I could stop crying," I whimpered, clumsily pushing LuLu aside.

"Pregnancy is a crazy time, huh?" He smiled at me compassionately and squeezed my shoulder as I nodded. "Let's get you home. Oh, wait… Food first. I don't think anyone can safely cook when they're crying, right?"

I gave him a grateful grin, and LuLu let out a deep sigh as she settled back down on my lap. Gavin drove to Snapper's Waterfront café, and then ran in to grab some take out burgers. While I waited for him to come back I mumbled to LuLu about how I might have made a terrible mistake by pushing Linc away, but right then I couldn't think straight. Crying all day had made me more tired than I wanted to really admit. I knew my hormones were to blame for most of my mood swings, but it really hurt when I thought about how Linc had wished on that star for me to have a baby. It didn't matter that his wish, and mine, had come true. Linc simply shouldn't have wished for something when he believed I couldn't give it to him. But hadn't *I* wished for the same thing when I knew I couldn't have a baby?

Gavin came back, and then drove me home. When I climbed out of the truck with LuLu, Gavin leaned across the seat.

"Want me to send any message along to Linc?"

I paused for a moment then shook my head. "No... I think we still need a little time apart before we talk. Just tell him... Tell him I'm okay."

Gavin grinned and nodded. He gave me his number and said goodnight, and then waited until LuLu and I were safely inside before he took off.

And then we were alone. The house was dark and all I could hear was the ticking of the clock and LuLu's paws padding across the kitchen to her food bowl. I put the burger down on the coffee table, and then fed my pup before I slumped down onto the couch in the dark. I felt empty and sad, and tears started to well up again as I remembered how warm and full I'd felt just the night before, when I was in Linc's arms...

LuLu jumped up on the couch and panted at me with gross dog-food breath, so I took that as a reason to get up and switch on the lights. It was way too quiet, so I flicked on the radio, listening to the love song dedication show while trying to remind myself that love existed in the world, and maybe, just maybe, love would return to me and make everything okay...

"I really think I messed this up, LuLu. I thought Linc was abandoning me, but then I went ahead and abandoned him! Does that make me an idiot?" LuLu just cocked her head to the side. "Yeah, I guess it does, but I really, really need to just have some space and get these pregnancy emotions under control. If I talk to Linc now, I may blow up on him again, and that's not going to help either of us."

I was halfway through my burger when I heard a familiar voice on the radio.

"I'd like to dedicate this song to Shawn."

I sat bolt upright and just about choked on my mouthful of food. It wasn't Linc's voice... It was Cole's.

"I miss him and so does my dad, and I hope he'll come back soon. This is for you, Shawn."

If my heart was breaking before, it was splitting apart into infinitely smaller pieces now. I lay back on the couch and clutched my chest as the first few notes of "Somewhere Out There" played, more tears welling up in my eyes.

I reached for my phone and almost called Linc before LuLu licked my hand. I looked at her and she coked her head to the side again.

"You're right. I did just say I needed some space to work this out. I'm way too raw to talk to him right now."

Instead, I called Gavin.

"Can you pass on a message for me?" I asked quickly when he answered.

"Sure, anything."

"Tell Cole I love him, and I'll see him again soon, no matter what happens with Linc and me."

"You heard the song, huh?" I heard the sly smile in Gavin's voice.

"Did you put him up to that?"

"No! Linc would kill me for interfering. I just know Linc told Cole you were a little upset and needed a few days to yourself."

"So, you listen to that particular love song radio show for your own enjoyment?" I was kind of joking, expecting Gavin to say he knew Cole was going to make a dedication to me, but then Gavin surprised me.

"Even us alphas have our guilty pleasures. Tell anyone and I'll never forgive you."

I chuckled, delighted to know he had a soft side for a man so large. Just like Linc in a way. "Your secret's safe with me."

"And your message is safe with me."

I thanked him then hung up with a sigh, and then went about dragging blankets to the couch, not wanting to smell Linc's scent on my pillows or feel the empty space beside me in bed where he should have been.

Chapter 17 - Linc

I was fed up. Enough was enough. A week had gone by since I'd last seen Shawn. Summer was upon us. The fresh, warm air was filled with the sound of mating birds and the impression of bourgeoning love. And where was my mate? Still not talking to me.

Gavin reported back to Jaxon and me that Shawn was miserable but he was still going to work, seemed in good health, and was even stargazing. But he sure wasn't replying to my texts. I'd sent so many I'd actually become quite poetic in an effort to not repeat myself outright. I'd also realized I could have been more understanding about Shawn's abandonment issues. Though I'd explained as best I could about my concerns over the claiming bite, I hadn't actually convinced him I had every intention of claiming him once the baby was born. I also could have been more considerate when he'd been upset about me wishing on that damn star. I just thought it was what *he* wanted. I loved Shawn exactly how he was, and now all I wanted was to show him—and to win him back.

I'm so sorry for hurting you.

Nothing in reply.

I wish I could take back everything I said. It was a misunderstanding, but I could have communicated better. You're the light of my life. I want to be with you forever. Please forgive me.

Silence.

I'll do whatever it takes to get you back. I miss you so much.

Dead air.

By day seven, I was even having nightmares about him ignoring me, and I woke up feeling painfully anxious. My wolf stalked back and forth inside me, frustrated and desperate to get its mate back. After rolling out of bed before dawn, I stumbled down the stairs, and then shifted into my wolf form at the back door. I ran right to Jaxon's house.

My pack leader, his mate and I sat in their kitchen while their perfect baby slept peacefully in the next room. Bryce had bags under his eyes and couldn't help but yawn every few minutes, and I apologized at least ten times for waking them up.

"It's fine," he insisted. "This is important. Besides, I'm really good at napping these days."

I chuckled and nodded, remembering what it was like raising a newborn cub when Cole was a baby. My heart ached when I thought about the unborn babe I wanted to raise, if only I could get Shawn back.

"I need your advice," I said. "What Shawn wants, I think, is to be part of the pack. To feel like I'm really, truly committed to him. That I accept him and I *won't* leave him. And I think the claiming ceremony is what he needs to show him that I'm all in."

Bryce was nodding so furiously that Jaxon and I raised our eyebrows at him.

"Well, duh. As an omega, I get it. Especially as someone who's been in his shoes as a human omega. He's on the outside of so much of your life, just by virtue of you being a completely different creature."

"Hey, we're not that different—"

"Yes, we are," Bryce insisted. "You are. From his perspective, the two of you really are very different. You have to remember he'd never heard of a wolf shifter before he met you. That's as foreign as it gets."

"Hm," I said, and considered Bryce's point. "I'd actually never thought of that. All of this must be really scary to him."

Jaxon nodded.

"Hell yeah," Bryce agreed. "And as a shifter, you come with this whole pack. It's not just your in-laws or your son's mom he has to fit in with. It's your entire community. He's an outsider until he becomes one of us. You're asking him to trust that you'll be there for him, but you haven't included him fully in your life."

"But the bite changes the human body. There aren't enough facts about pregnant humans receiving the bite. What if he accidentally shifts..." I shuddered. The unborn baby, though a shifter, couldn't shift in uterus if its mother or father shifted. Could it?

"It's never been documented that it's ever happened," Jaxon said as calmly as he could.

"Sure, but I need to fully understand the risk if he does," I insisted.

"What did Maddie say when you asked her?" he asked.

"That she'd never heard of any complications."

"See?" Jaxon smiled as if that was settled.

"Yes, but—"

"I think you need to talk to her again," Bryce said. "Really explain your concerns."

I glanced at Jaxon, who sighed, but I knew he understood. "Fine, I'll call her." He made a quick phone call and within ten minutes, Maddie Reed walked into the living room, carrying a doctor's bag.

"Everything okay with Lori?" she asked.

"Just fine, thanks, Maddie. She's an angel," Jaxon said. "There's someone else here who needs your help."

I waved and grinned sheepishly, suddenly embarrassed that she'd come all this way just for me.

"Lincoln," she said in acknowledgment. "Is Shawn okay?"

"As far as I know." God, it felt awful saying that. I was supposed to be taking care of my mate, making sure he was safe and well looked after, and I hadn't seen him in a week. I'd basically abandoned him, exactly what he'd been afraid of.

Maddie raised her brow, and I felt guilt heat the back of my neck.

"You've had a fight," she said. "About the claiming bite, haven't you? I know Shawn wanted to be claimed, and I know you've not done it yet, and the fact that you've called me means you're still worried about how it will affect him. Right?"

I nodded, barely able to look her in the eye. "It's just..." I cleared my throat. "I mean... We know he shouldn't be able to shift while he's pregnant. But what if something happens and he does?"

"It's a biological impossibility. The worst that could happen is Shawn may feel lightheaded or dizzy. How did you feel, Bryce?"

"Fine. Better than fine actually," Bryce said.

"But just because—"

"Linc, I understand your concerns, I do, but the bite will not affect Shawn adversely, and it absolutely won't hurt the baby. I told you this."

"Yes, I know. I just…"

"You were worried, just like any good alpha should be about his omega, so let me explain something else, so you have all the facts on the table. Pregnancy always comes with risks. Nicole had a really easy time with Cole as I recall it, so you might not be aware of how things *can* go wrong, but ultimately they usually turn out fine."

"It's the *usually* I'm worried about," I mumbled.

"Taking the claiming bite off the table because that isn't an issue, if Shawn were to have any other normal health issues that puts a pregnancy into a high risk category, we would immediately put him on bedrest and observation. There are protocols to deal with these things, and plenty of tests we could run to assess the health of the baby, and of Shawn. You have an entire team of wolf shifter medical staff, myself included, who would be giving him top medical care—and Shawn would have the entire hospital staff waiting on him hand and foot, I'm sure. You would really have nothing, or very little, to worry about."

I realized I'd been holding my breath and let it out in one, long gust. "What the hell have I been so worried about then?" I shook my head then groaned, covering my face with my hands.

Jaxon chuckled and put a hand on my back, patting me gently. "Don't beat yourself up about it. Like Maddie said, it's your job to worry."

"Actually, not everyone knows this, or wants to admit it, but pregnancy hormones actually affect both parents," Maddie said with a smug smile.

I growled in resistance to that idea, but I had to admit it made a lot of sense. I'd been on edge since Shawn had told me he was pregnant.

"Thanks, Maddie," Jaxon said warmly. "I think that's all we needed to know."

"My pleasure." She smiled then stood and gathered her things. Jaxon went to show her out, but she stopped for a moment and said, "Call me, Linc. Seriously, any time you have a concern. It can help to talk to a professional."

I grinned and waved, not wanting to promise I would, but glad of the offer.

When Jaxon returned to sit with us, I took a deep breath and grimaced. "I should have listened to her the first time around. Now I may have ruined my chance with Shawn."

"I doubt it. Gavin has been keeping me informed, and he said Shawn looks miserable, and it's obvious he misses you."

"He hasn't been answering any of my texts…"

"But he's been talking to Cole."

My heart thumped. "He has? How do you know?"

"Cole told Liam, and Liam told us. Apparently Shawn has been asking Cole about you."

"So why hasn't Cole said anything about it to me?"

"I don't know. Better talk to your son," Bryce said, putting a hand on my knee and squeezing it in sympathy and understanding.

I groaned again, realizing how much of a fuck up I'd made of this.

"So, are you ready to claim Shawn now?" Jaxon asked directly.

I looked at him, and then at Bryce. My wolf pawed at my chest more than ready for me to claim my mate. I swallowed, and then nodded. "Hell yes. I need to get my mate back."

***

I picked up Cole from school and filled him in on the plan, though I didn't question him about his conversations with Shawn or why he hadn't told me. I suppose he would eventually, and it must have been hard for him to be pulled between loyalties like that. I knew Cole loved Shawn as much as he loved me.

He bounced in the back seat and let out a series of excited howls as we made our way home, where we set up an extra surprise before we headed out to the Lodge. By the time we got there, half the pack had gathered and everyone was busy decorating the hall, setting up seating, and hauling in booze.

"How did you manage to get all of this done so soon?" I asked.

"Alpha's orders," Jaxon said as he wrapped an arm around my shoulder.

"And hey, we love to welcome a new member to the pack," Gavin added as he walked up to us, hauling a case of beer under his arm.

"Shit, I hope this works." I looked around at the spectacle they'd put together. The rafters were covered in gold, flowing silk that had been embroidered by members of our pack hundreds of years ago. Tables lined the hall, decked with flowers and carved stone statues. Jaxon had put on a show when he'd claimed Bryce, but I think this beat it, hands down, but then perhaps I was biased.

Gavin slapped my back. "If my time listening to sappy love songs has taught me anything, it's that a grand gesture like this always works."

I swallowed nervously and felt my wolf whimper inside me. "I sure hope you're right."

Cole and I helped with the rest of the set-up, hauling in furniture and setting up the sound system. The manual labor kept my mind calm, and eventually, my nerves were under control.

Cole was speaking loudly into a microphone for the sound test when Jaxon pulled me aside.

"Gavin and Nicole have just picked up Shawn from work. Gavin said Shawn was reluctant to 'come for dinner', but he's coming anyway… They're getting LuLu, then heading straight here," he said.

My stomach churned and my heart started racing. I took a deep breath and put a hand on Jaxon's shoulder to support myself. "What if he says no? What if he won't take me back?"

"We've got you," he said, putting a hand on the small of my back and leading me outside. I swallowed and nodded while letting him lead me through the front doors of the Lodge. The sun had almost disappeared and the tops of the trees looked jet black against the dusky twilight sky. The outside of the Lodge was strung up with fairy lights and lanterns, and the road was lined with fire torches, all the way to the gate of the homestead.

My wolf whined nervously as I watched the glow of headlights coming into view at the gates. As they drew closer, I listened to the crunch of the tires and knew it was Gavin's car. I held my breath and was about to step forward, out of Jaxon's grip, when I felt a tugging on my sleeve. I looked down and found it was Cole.

"Dad," Cole said quietly, holding up a big bouquet of flowers he grabbed off one of the tables. "You should give this to Shawn."

My heart almost broke into a million pieces at how precious he was. "Thanks, kiddo," I said, wiping away a tear then taking the flowers from him. He gave me a big cheesy grin, and then stood behind Jaxon's legs. Jax chuckled and gave me a slap on the back.

The car pulled up and I could barely see through the glass, but my heart fluttered when I thought I caught a glimpse of a silhouette of Shawn's profile in the back window. My legs felt weak and my stomach was churning while time moved slowly. I watched as Nicole hopped out of the passenger side door before going to open the back door. One at a time, Shawn's feet hit the ground—ground that would rightfully belong to him too, if he accepted my proposal. An instant later, he appeared.

My wolf lunged forward. I stumbled, almost fell, and hurried over to him.

"Linc—" He covered his mouth as he took in the lights and beauty of the Lodge. "Linc, this is—"

Before he could go on, I held out the flowers... And dropped to one knee.

Chapter 18 - Shawn

I had to remind myself to breathe. Linc was on one knee, the Lodge was lit up like it was Disneyland, and my stomach was fluttering like I was about to get on a highspeed rollercoaster. I looked down at the man who had given me so much grief over the last week. I had missed him, really missed him, but his texts simply hadn't been enough for me to forgive him, but this... As our eyes met, my heart ached, and I wanted to throw myself into his arms. He looked at me, not only with genuine remorse, but a whole lot of true love.

"I'm so sorry for being stupid and saying all the wrong things," he said, his voice sincere.

I lowered my hands and slowly took the bouquet he held out. "This is a lot of effort for a simple apology," I said as I sniffed at the roses.

Linc grinned and nodded then held out his left hand. I looked down and wet my lips. Was he serious?

"If you can forgive me I want to show you how much I love you. I always have, and though I haven't really shown it in the past, I will always be here for you. So, Shawn Drocella, my love, my mate, may I claim you tonight?"

As our hands touched, I felt light headed. I'd been holding my breath again, and as I remembered to exhale, it came out as a high-pitched squeal. "Yes!" I cried, barely able to contain my excitement.

Linc planted a single kiss on the back of my left hand, then stood and threw his arms around me. The bouquet was crushed between us, sending up a waft of rose that made me even more lightheaded. I let myself melt into the hug, and reveled in the feeling of my baby bump pressing against my baby's daddy.

"Oh, Linc, I missed you so much," I whispered as I pushed my face against his neck and took in his smell.

"I've been lost without you," he mumbled.

I pulled back and pressed my lips against his in a soft, needy kiss before looking up at him seriously. "What changed your mind about the ceremony?"

"Being without you was too much to bear," he said quietly. "Also, I spoke to Jaxon and Bryce, who insisted I talk to Maddie again. She put my fears to rest once and for all."

I spotted Jaxon silhouetted by the bright lights streaming out from the Lodge's doorway. He had a huge smile on his face, and Cole was peeking out from behind his legs. Suddenly, the kid ran over and hugged me around my belly.

"Hey Cole!" I said, crouching down and pulling him into a proper hug. "I missed you."

He squeezed me tight. "I missed you too. Then he looked up at his dad. "Um, Dad, I've been talking to Shawn and—"

Linc nodded. "I know, and that's fine. Thank you for telling me."

"I played him a song on the radio as well." Cole's face turned a little pink, and then he buried his face in my neck. I looked over his shoulder and found Linc beaming at us, his arm around Jaxon's shoulder. The pack leader smiled at me warmly, and he held his arms out to me as I stood and led Cole over to them.

I hugged Jaxon and I felt something stirring deep in my heart as he welcomed me to the pack.

"We're so happy you want to join us," he said.

"Thank you for accepting me."

He nodded, and then stood back as Linc threaded my arm through the crook in his. The two of us stepped into the Lodge, and I gasped. Again I felt so light headed I needed to hold tightly to Linc's arm. The large hall was decorated with elaborate florals; it was like walking into a spring greenhouse. The rafters were strewn with ivy, hollyhock and grape vines. Bunches of full, richly-scented roses dotted the greenery, and the whole room smelled heady. Long, communal tables with benches spanned the hall and cascading displays of flowers and fairy lights billowed down their middles as center pieces. I placed my slightly crushed bouquet on the nearest table, and it immediately blended in with the overabundance of spray roses.

I turned to Linc and could barely see him for the tears that welled in my eyes. "Linc, this is beautiful."

"It's all for you," he said, leaning over and pressing his lips against my cheek.

"I can't... I can't believe..." I looked out at the pack who was about to become my family. Everyone was hurrying around, fixing up finishing touches. Kids were laughing and chasing each other through the aisles, wielding flowers and breadsticks like swords. Even people I'd never met, who knew nothing about me, were here, putting in work to make my special day even more special. I put a hand on my chest and took a deep breath. It was exactly the type of community I had always wanted to be part of.

***

After I'd changed into the tuxedo Linc had got me, which fitted over my baby bump perfectly, Linc and I stood under an arbor of bright red roses within a crescent of oversized ceremonial candles. The lights of the hall had been dimmed, and we were in the spotlight of the flames' radiance. Linc, his face softened under the orange glow, looked like a hopeful young boy, and the eagerness in his eyes tugged at my heart. The pack had crowded in close around us, but everyone was quiet and attentive.

Jaxon stepped into the crescent of candles and took his place behind us. Linc reached out and took my hands, and I felt his fingers trembling just as nervously as mine were. We shared a shy smile as Jaxon cleared his throat and began the ceremony.

"We are here to accept our friend, Shawn Drocella, as a wolf shifter of the Timberwood Pack," he announced, and I felt a shiver roll up my spine.

"Shawn has come to us as the fated mate of our own much-loved Lincoln Travers. The connection between the two of them is undeniable, and I invite the couple to now share heartfelt words before we commence the ceremony."

I felt light headed again, and again I remembered to breathe. My heart thudded, and the roar of my pulse in my ears almost drowned out what Linc was saying.

"I've loved you since the very first moment I saw you," he said, then he cleared his throat as his voice broke. "Which means I've loved you before I even really knew you. But knowing you as I do now, I love you even more. I can't wait to learn more about you as we grow old together... And I can't wait to meet your wolf!"

A loud howl of excitement came from the back of the crowd and the pack laughed before quickly quieting down. I smiled and felt my cheeks flushing as I remembered that so many eyes were on me.

"I..." I shook my head, stuck finding the words. "There's... Oh, there's just so much I want to say!"

Linc squeezed my hands encouragingly.

"We didn't give him much time to prepare," Jaxon explained, and the crowd chuckled in understanding.

I swallowed nervously and looked down at my hands, holding tightly to Linc's. If I imagined it was just him and me in this beautifully decorated room, maybe I could squeak out a few words...

"I love you, Linc. Part of me is still in disbelief that wolf shifters exist—even after meeting so many of you! But those feelings of disbelief are nowhere near as strong as my desire to be with you... I want to be with you, Linc. Tied to you, bonded to you—forever." I looked up from our joined hands and saw tears streaking down Linc's face. A sob escaped my lips as felt my own tears starting to trickle down my cheeks.

"Let's began," Jaxon said, and the pack cheered.

Linc beamed at me, and we stepped closer to each other. I felt the energy in the air beginning to change. I nervously touched the spot on my neck where Linc was going to bite me. Bryce had assured me that any pain I felt would fade as quickly as my wolf came into my body, but I wasn't so sure... I glanced around nervously as Linc stepped closer and held me in his arms.

"Are you ready?" he whispered.

My heart pounded.

"Are you ready, Shawn?"

I glanced around at the pack again, these people who were shifters, all of whom were looking at me eagerly. Linc touched my cheek and drew my gaze back to him. As our eyes met, all of my fear melted away. My alpha was here, right here with me, and I knew I was completely safe with him. I'd follow him anywhere.

"I'm ready," I said. Linc gave me one more reassuring smile and pulled me in close.

"I love you," Linc said close to my ear, and I immediately tilted my neck back, exposing the skin for him to bite. I squeezed my eyes shut and held my breath, waiting for the pain.

A tiny sting flushed across my neck and then faded to nothing. I waited. Everything was quiet. I was about to open my eyes to see what had gone wrong, when it appeared to me...

Out of the darkness behind my eyes, a wolf approached me. Its thick fur was stark white with gray patches along its back, flank, and its lengthy, thin legs. Its snout was long and defined, and its nose was velvety black. As it grew closer I caught its gaze. Suddenly, a shock of recognition moved through me and I almost fell over. Its eyes were the same as mine. It was like looking in the mirror, deep into my own self.

It sat before me and lowered its head in greeting. I moved forward and ran a hand over the top of its head. It felt warm and strong, and I liked how it made *me* feel strong. It looked up, and I knelt to run my hands over its jaw and its thick, beautiful neck.

"Wow," I whispered.

My wolf lapped at my neck where I'd received my bite, and the next thing I knew, it was nudging its head against my chest, softly at first, and then with all its strength. I stumbled backward, not sure what it wanted. The wolf growled, baring its teeth, and nudged me again. I was two seconds away from panicking when I remembered something else Bryce had said. This was my wolf, and I commanded it.

"Stop!" I ordered.

It immediately looked up at me and our eyes connected. Again, I was shocked I was looking at *myself*. But the wolf did exactly what I told it to. After a second it whined, and this time I knew what it wanted.

"Alright," I whispered, accepting my wolf. "Come in."

I closed my eyes, surrendered to the push, and let my wolf become part of me.

When I opened my eyes, Linc was staring down at me.

"Am I..." I whispered, half delirious.

Linc laughed and planted a kiss on my cheek. "Yes, the claiming bite took. Did you feel your wolf?"

"Yes, it's inside me now. I can feel him." I touched my chest in awe, then smiled up at Linc. Then I wrapped my hands around my swollen stomach. "Wow, I can feel my cub too, it's as if our bond is stronger now."

Linc nodded. "I felt your wolf come to life, and we all bonded."

"That's kind of amazing," I said.

"Yeah, it is."

Slowly, I became aware of the pack surrounding us. Jaxon wrapped an arm around both of us and spoke to me. "Welcome to the pack."

I laughed and smiled at him in gratitude, then Linc and I made our way through the crowd, accepting gifts and words of congratulations for our relationship and my initiation. Cole held LuLu's leash, but she pulled toward me to give her own congratulations. I crouched down and hugged her, letting her lick my chin, and she panted happily. I smiled up at Linc, grateful he'd allowed her to be a part of the ceremony.

Then the party really started. Linc and I ate at the long, decorated tables with everyone else, with Cole next to us and Liam beside him. Bryce and Jaxon sat opposite us, and Gavin and Nicole beside them. The whole hall was full of laughter, cheer, and music, and the feast was delicious with fresh flavors and light seasoning. I could taste more details about the food than I'd ever noticed before.

"This is delicious," I moaned as I bit into forkful of green beans.

"Your senses are sharpening," Jaxon explained.

"And it *is* delicious," Bryce insisted. "Most of us on the homestead use a lot of foraged foods from the forests. You'll get some really unique flavor combinations living here."

Linc visibly kicked Bryce's shin under the table. "Don't pressure him."

I shook my head and wrapped my arm around Linc's shoulder. "That's okay, I think it's only right for me to move in with you, don't you?"

"God yes, and I have a surprise at home for you too."

***

After everyone had left the party and we'd all cleaned up, Linc drove Cole and I home in his truck. As we passed through the homestead, I looked out the window at the dark woods behind it, and I felt a part deep inside me stirring.

"I feel like I already know this place," I said softly. "Like I belong."

Linc glanced over at me and took my hand. "The homestead?"

"Yeah, maybe my wolf finds it familiar..." I said, smiling at Linc. "I guess it's because its packmates are from here."

"What's your wolf like, Shawn?" Cole asked as he stuck his head through the middle of the seats.

"Sit back," Linc growled, shoving his son back without taking his eyes off the road.

I turned in my seat and craned my neck to talk to Cole.

"White, and gray, and strong," I said, as my wolf sat up with its ears pricked, happy for the attention.

"Strong, huh?" Linc glanced at me with a sparkle of pride in his eyes.

"Yep, super strong," I said.

"Cool," Cole said. "Can I see it later? Do you want to go for a run?"

Suddenly, my wolf started clawing in my chest at the idea of getting to run. I smiled because I couldn't wait until I was able, to see the world through my wolf's eyes.

"No, Cole. Shawn can't shift yet. Not until the baby is born, and then he has to learn, like Liam did."

"Oh. Okay, well, when you're able to, can we go for a run then?"

"Of course, buddy. As soon as I learn." However, I didn't think it was going to take me long, not with the way my wolf was pacing.

Linc pulled up to the house, parked the car, and then got out to open my door for me. I gratefully took his hand and let him lead me through the front door. Cole immediately hugged us goodnight and raced to his bedroom with LuLu in tow, allegedly to get some good sleep.

"He's actually been stargazing from the roof every night," Linc said. "I'm not sure why he feels the need to cover it up."

"Maybe it's more fun as a secret," I said. "I used to do that, when I was a kid. It felt more magical that way."

"Really?" Linc asked, sounding like he was impressed.

"Yeah! Didn't you have any secrets as a kid?"

"Of course I did. I still have a lot of secrets, actually," he said with a smirk, then he took my hand.

A shiver of excitement thrilled me as we headed up the stairs, and I wondered what he could be about to show me. I eyed him as he walked in front of me; his plump ass, his muscular back, his strong shoulders. I couldn't wait to see him without all of those clothes on again, despite how good he looked in a tux. I'd missed his body so much.

When we got to the top of the stairs, he slipped behind me and put his hands over my eyes.

"Mm," I said, pushing my ass back against his crotch. He growled in my ear and steered me down the hallway. Instead of turning right into the bedroom, we made a sudden left.

"Hang on, keep your eyes closed for a moment okay?"

"Okay…" I said. My imagination was going wild with ideas of what Linc might be about to show me… My wolf paced again, like it was just as excited to find out what we were in for. Was Linc changing into some kind of sexy outfit? I giggled thinking about him wearing chaps, but then my mind went to ideas of him tying me up with a lasso, and my cock started getting a little hard.

"Alright, ready!" he said from behind me, and I saw a bright light turn on through my eyelids. I flicked my eyes open, and my heart completely melted.

"Linc! What?" I cried out, covering my face with my hands.

"Do you like it?" he asked, coming up beside me and pulling me into a tight hug.

I was speechless. I looked through my fingers at the incredible, elegant nursery he had decorated. The walls were painted a deep navy blue with gold trim, and on the back wall was a gigantic mural of the night sky, complete with real constellations. The whole room was furnished with unique pieces, including a beautiful pine crib with intricate carved headboard featuring two large wolves and two cubs.

"You did all of this?" I whispered, barely able to believe it.

Linc looked down and grinned, clearly pleased with himself but also trying to seem humble.

"This is so incredible," I said, walking around the room while tracing my hands over the beautiful furniture.

"I made the crib," he mumbled, and I gasped at him.

"Are you serious?".

He nodded, biting down on his bottom lip and smiling.

"Linc, this is amazing. Like...mind-blowing. I'm so... I'm so..." I started to get tears in my eyes and quickly wiped them away.

"Cole helped me with the constellations," he admitted. "And the mobile." He pointed to the crib, and I saw an adorable mobile of felt wolves, stars, and moons hovering above it.

"So sweet." I smiled and came back to stand beside my man as I admired the room he'd created for our cub. Suddenly, I slapped his arm. "I thought it was going to be a sexy secret!"

Linc laughed and quickly kissed me. "I have one of those for you too."

"Really?" I raised my eyebrows, and he laughed.

"No, but let's make some secrets together." He smirked, and then suddenly raced down the hall.

"Hey no fair!" I sighed, and then I waddled down the hall as fast as I could.

I caught up to him in the bedroom, and within minutes I was naked and falling onto the bed. I was immediately taken over by total instinct. As I pushed my tongue into Linc's mouth, my mind fell blank, and the silence of my thoughts was blissful. All I was aware of was the feeling of his hands on my belly, the taste of his saliva, and the sound of his breath and moans that made the hair on the back of my neck stand on end. I shivered with desire as I ran my hands through his full hair then traced them over his shoulders, his strong arms, and his slim waist. I reached for everything I wanted to touch. I couldn't hold back. My cock was already aching and hard, and a drop of precum spilled out from the tip when he wrapped his palm around the base. I moaned and pushed my hips back and forth to fuck his hand, completely absorbed by his mouth and his touch.

"You're wild," he whispered in my ear.

"You're mine," I whispered back before playfully nipping at his neck. He groaned and pushed me off, pinned me down, and then bit at my bottom lip while lowering his hips so our dicks were pressed alongside each other. My cock jerked at the contact, and Linc let out a hot moan before starting to thrust his cock against mine. I looked up and saw his expression—the same look he'd given me the first time we'd ever made love.

Without warning, he lifted my legs over his shoulders and positioned me so his cock was pressed right against my sopping wet hole. Even I could smell my slick, and I wasn't surprised when he took a long, deep inhale as he spread my legs wider. He growled low in his throat, and then pushed inside.

"Fuck!"

"You like it?" he asked before thrusting in another inch. My hole twitched and throbbed, aching to take more of his length.

"Y-yes!" I arched my back and wriggled my hips to get more of him inside me.

Linc grunted and gave me about half of his cock. I panted as a shock of pleasure burst through me. Linc gripped my thighs tighter, pulling back before sliding the entire length of his thick cock into me until he bottomed out.

I let out a cry and Linc quickly grabbed a pillow for me to bite down on, lest I make too much noise. The last thing I wanted was for Cole to hear us. I giggled, then bit down dutifully as I looked up at Linc's face set in desire. In reaction my hole tightened, and he let out a pleased groan as he pulled back through the tightness.

My eyes locked onto Linc's, and I held my breath as a surge of energy moved between us, like a tingling, throbbing wave. Linc looked down at me, and a sly smirk spread across his lips a moment before he began moving; pulling his hips back, and then pushing forward until his cock was all the way up to the hilt again.

"Oh f-fuck," I whimpered into the pillow, clutching it to my chest and struggling to keep my eyes open and locked on his. A buzzing, throbbing vibration of pleasure started to spread from my hole up through my cock. My balls pulled up tight and I felt my dick twitch with every thrust he made inside me. Linc panted as he fucked me hard, his own eyes closing as he dug his fingers deeper into my thighs.

"Take my cock," he said, thrusting harder and faster. "Take it, Shawn."

He thrust so deep inside me I was barely able to hold myself in one place. I had one hand wrapped in a sheet, the other now clutching Linc's bicep. He continued to pound in and out of my soaking wet hole, and a muffled, desperate groan escaped my throat. My mind was completely taken by the rhythm of his thrusts, and I could barely believe I was being fucked this passionately. I could practically feel Linc's desire being pummeled into me. I struggled for breath as all the pleasure that had built inside now began to spread throughout my entire body. Linc's eyes were rolling back, and he was lost in his pleasure, gripping my thighs hard and thrusting even harder. My dick throbbed and throbbed again. I bit down on the pillow and groaned as quietly as I could as my balls pulled up, my cock spasmed, and I started to come.

I lost control of my hips, trying to grind myself on Linc's cock as my orgasm rocked through me. My dick shot thick ropes of cum against the underside of my stretched belly, and the heat from it made me shiver in pleasure. That's when Linc suddenly pulled out. I let out a whimper of protest, but watched as Linc squatted between my legs and grabbed his cock, shining wet and literally dripping with my slick. He quickly slid his hand along the length, and then, with his other hand, he rubbed the cum from my orgasm over my bump.

"You're so fucking hot," he said, smearing the fluid over my tight, bulging belly. I was fixated on watching him jerking off his cock, his grip slipping down to the base and back up again in one easy movement. However, Linc seemed fixated on rubbing my big belly. Then he squeezed the head of his cock and threw his head back, letting out a pained groan while clenching his jaw. Streams of cum jetted from his cock and landed all over my belly. Linc caught his breath and watched, barely keeping himself upright as he sprayed all over me. By the time he was spent, I was completely saturated in his cum.

He collapsed beside me, but still kept one hand on my stomach. "Wow."

"That was... Yep," I agreed between pants, and then I chuckled. Linc leaned over and kissed me, soft and with all the love I knew he had for me. "I'm so sorry for doubting you, for doubting the way you felt about me. It's not an excuse, but I guess my hormones completely took hold and everything seemed so overwhelming that I couldn't grasp what was real and what wasn't."

"You don't have to apologize, Shawn. I made a mistake in not trusting what my pack was telling me. I just became super cautious. I couldn't stand the thought of anything happening to you..."

"Yeah, I get that now, but everything is fine, right?"

"Yes, babe, everything is fine." Linc kissed me again, and I honestly never wanted him to stop.

"This was the best day of my life," I said when he eventually pulled back.

Linc smiled at me and shook his head. "The best is yet to come," he said.

I raised my eyebrows. "You think that hot shower I'm about to take is going to top that?"

Linc laughed, and the deep baritone moved through me like a warm hug.

"Not that," he said with a smile. "Something even better."

He possessively stroked along my bump. My heart surged, and I wrapped my arms around his neck, pulling him down for another sweet, deep kiss. I felt giddy and excited to start my new life here with my mate and our new cub. And he was right. So much was still to come.

Chapter 19 - Linc

"*No*, Dad! *This* is the blackhole. *That's* Andromeda!"

"My mistake! They're both black," I grumbled as I peered at the intricate—and, frankly, incredible—space model that Cole had made for his school's September Science Fair. Cole rolled his eyes and shot Shawn a glance that said he was tired of dealing with "space fools" as he'd started calling anyone who didn't understand what he thought was basic space stuff. I would have been offended if he hadn't looked so cute in his galaxy-print bow tie and pint-sized lab coat.

"I'm going to win this competition," he stated with the tiniest shake of nervousness in his voice.

"Who do you think is your biggest competition?" Shawn asked as he put an arm around Cole's shoulders and looked out across the playground where the rest of the science fair exhibits were set up.

"Oh my god, Liam for sure! His display is so cool!" Cole grabbed his face and made a sound like he was in excruciating pain.

"What did he make?" I asked, at risk of sounding like a space fool again.

"He wanted to do a wolf shifter in space, but Jaxon wouldn't let him."

"Well, yeah," I said. "So what *did* he do?"

"Like…a UFO! It has LED lights that get bright in different patterns depending on its mood."

"Its *mood*?"

Cole rolled his eyes again, and I looked at Shawn who gave me a shrug that said he had no idea how a UFO could have a *mood* either. At least I wasn't the only space fool for once.

"The judges are coming," Cole said excitedly, smoothing down the front of his white lab coat before shooting us a look to tell us to get the hell out of there. "I don't want them thinking you helped me out."

"Alright," I said, holding my hands up defensively, even though we hadn't helped him. Shawn had let him use his telescope and look at his books on space, but the whole model was all Cole's doing.

Shawn and I shuffled off, and I do mean *shuffled*. Shawn was heavily pregnant and ready to pop at any minute. If I'd been attracted to his big belly three months earlier, I was completely obsessed with it now. I couldn't keep my hands off it at home, and I spoke to our unborn son almost as much as I spoke to Shawn. In public, I managed to keep myself under control, though my eyes kept flicking to his protruding bump as we walked toward the auditorium then took our seats near the stage, waiting for the awards to begin.

"Hey, lovers," Nicole said as she slid into a seat next to me and gave us both kisses on our cheeks. "Did you see our kiddo's model?"

Paco sat at her feet and sniffed at my hand, probably looking for traces of LuLu.

"It looks like something out of a sci-fi game," Gavin declared as he leaned over from the other side of Nicole and gave us a thumbs up. "He's gonna win, no question."

I glanced around and found Jaxon at the back, bouncing Lori in his arms. Bryce came into view and gave me a little wave and a thumbs-up. I returned the gesture and Nicole elbowed my side.

"Don't be nice to the enemy," she hissed. "They're our competition right now!"

I laughed and nudged her back. Shawn fanned himself with the program and blew air out of pursed lips.

"Feeling okay?" I asked, putting my hand on his forehead. Since the claiming bite, he hadn't had any more severe morning sickness and the rest of the pregnancy had been fairly symptom-free, but the last few weeks he'd been hot and bothered.

"It's fine," he insisted, resting a hand on my knee and squeezing it. "Look, it's starting."

We all sat back and listened as best we could to the school principal droning on about the science program, until the lead science teacher finally introduced the judges. I caught Cole's eye from his place to the right of the stage where the kids stood with their models. I gave him a wink and watched as he beamed, then stuck his tongue out at me.

"Cole Travers!" the judge announced.

Cole did a double-take, and so did I. He looked up at the stage and then looked at Liam, who was beaming and nodding.

"Cole Travers?" the judge said again. "First place!"

Cole grinned, and the audience exploded with applause as he bounded up the stairs to accept the award. I immediately stood, applauding loudly and whistling. Gavin let out a whoop, Paco barked, and Nicole let out a cheeky howl. We sat back down and let the cheering subside as Cole began to speak into the microphone.

"My name is Cole Travers and this is my diagram of all the known objects and phenomi—uh, *phenomenon* we know is in space," he said, and I my heart filled with pride.

"Um… Linc," Shawn said.

I glanced at him and found he was looking a little panicked.

"It's maybe not fine," he whispered.

"What? What's happening? Is the baby?"

"Yes. It's, um, it's fine but it's happening. I think I'm going into labor."

I shot back to my feet. The scraping of my chair rocked through the auditorium and all eyes were on us as I helped Shawn to stand. Nicole, Paco, and Gavin sprang up to help us through the aisle. Cole had fallen silent. I looked up at him and gave him a nod to encourage him to keep going with his speech. But as we hurried through the auditorium, I heard Cole clear his throat.

"Thank you for the award, but I have to go help my dads now!" He dropped his model and raced off the stage to join us as we left through the large doors. Applause erupted through the auditorium as we spilled out into the soft fall light.

Jaxon and Bryce were right behind us as we stumbled toward my truck.

"I can't get in the truck, no way, it's too high." Shawn shook his head and let out a pained sigh.

"I'll get our car," Jaxon said, handing Lori to Bryce and quickly rushing off to the other side of the parking lot.

Shawn tried to smile in appreciation but let out a pained groan and doubled-over. I rushed forward but I had no idea whether to touch him or let him be. My legs were shaking and my wolf was pacing back and forth, on high alert, ears back and nose sniffing violently at the air. Paco sat still for once, looking on with a worried expression.

"Breathe through the contraction, that's it, breathe," Nicole said in encouragement as she stepped in front of me and started rubbing Shawn's back. He visibly relaxed under her touch. "This is normal. This is good. Everything's happening just right."

Cole raced up to my side and wrapped his arms around my hips.

"Is the baby okay?" he asked quietly.

I looked to Nicole who gave me a warm smile and reassuring nod.

"It's fine, Shawn's going into labor and he's going to have the baby soon," I told him, then I reached out and rubbed Shawn's back, following Nicole's lead. He gave me a warm, appreciative smile and I felt for a moment like I knew what I was doing.

"Yes! Brother time!" Cole said, pumping his fist in the air.

"How about you and I drive Paco home, then head over to the hospital in Dad's truck? We can get everything ready for Shawn," Nicole said to Cole, and I happily handed her the keys.

"You'll be fine," she whispered to me. "It's just like how it was with Cole."

"That was over a decade ago," I whispered back. "I'm not prepared!"

"Then it's lucky you're not the one going into labor." She laughed and slapped me on the back before heading for the truck with Cole and Paco. Gavin, Bryce and Lori went with them, and I stayed with Shawn, rubbing his back and encouraging him to breathe in the calmest voice I could muster. Admittedly, it wasn't very calm. I hated seeing him in pain, and every groan he let out made me feel like I was on high alert, ready to defend my mate.

Fighting the trembling in my hands, I helped Shawn into Jaxon's car, and then clambered into the backseat with him. I held his hand and counted out his breaths as our pack leader drove us across town to the hospital.

"Can you hurry?" I asked Jaxon.

"I got Maddie on the phone earlier," he called back to us from the driver's seat. "She said the delivery room will be ready for you, and not to freak out because these things usually take hours."

"Hours? I don't remember Cole's birth taking hours."

"Yeah, well, Lori took a long time comin' but I remember it as being two seconds. The mind has a way of shortening high stress situations."

"It's fine, darling." Shawn chuckled, patting my hand. "It really does take hours. I just need you to keep me calm and—oh god! Ouch! Shit! Shit!"

"This is the first time I've ever heard you swear, Shawn," Jaxon said, laughing.

"Well... Shit!" Shawn yelled, and Jaxon howled. I couldn't help but let out a loud laugh. It broke the tension and we hooted and howled until we pulled up to the hospital.

Maddie met us at the door with a wheelchair. "It'll help to speed things along if we walk, but we can use the chair if you need it," she said.

Shawn shook his head and waddled forward, taking Maddie's arm. She took him in, and Jaxon slapped my back, wished me luck, and went to wait in the waiting room. I took a deep breath and followed close behind my mate and his doctor, telling my wolf to keep calm and just stay out of the way.

But the moment we stepped into the hospital, I was hit with that *smell* and my wolf grumbled uncomfortably. I swallowed my nausea and focused on why I was there—I was going to greet my newborn son, and I'd just have to suck it up until then.

Nurses rushed over from their posts and got Shawn set up in the delivery room so quickly he was already on the table and hooked up to monitors and an IV before I'd gotten my scrubs on. When I walked in, he immediately burst out laughing.

"What? Did they give you the pain killers already?"

He giggled. "No, you just look so cute! The hair net really adds something," he said, reaching up and tugging at it.

I growled and grabbed his hand, bringing it to my lips and kissing it gently. He beamed at me as I sat beside him and pushed his hair back from his beautiful, glowing face.

"You're doing so good," I told him. "I'm so damn proud of you."

Shawn smiled, his eyes filling up with tears. I wiped them away. "Don't cry now. We can both do that when our son his born."

"Alright, team," Maddie said as she came into the room. "How are we doing?"

"Contractions are about four minutes apart," Shawn said.

"How are you so certain?" I asked. Shawn looked at me like I was a bit dumb.

"I'm a nurse."

"Still quite some time to go then," Maddie said. "And we're still adamant on having a natural birth?"

Shawn nodded fiercely.

"Alright, let's see how far along you are then," she said, slipping on a glove and lifting up the sheet that covered Shawn's legs.

He turned his head to look at me and gave me a cheeky grin, then whispered, "Jealous?"

I almost choked and barely stopped myself from bursting out laughing. He smiled smugly at having made me crack, and then looked up at the ceiling as Maddie checked how far he was dilated.

"Yes, you'll be a while yet," she declared, snapping off the glove and throwing it in the trash. "I'll have my team keep an eye on you, and I'll be right down the hall if you need anything. Just stay comfortable and breathe through the contractions."

Shawn gave her an appreciative smile, but I kept my eyes on him. He'd helped me calm down with his jokes, but my wolf was still on high alert. Regardless of how all of Shawn's check-ups had proved everything was going fine, I wouldn't know for certain until I held my baby in my arms.

Hours dragged by. I got more anxious by the second, and Shawn spent a lot of his time reassuring me, which helped but left me feeling guilty. At least the intense emotions overshadowed everything else, and I was able to ignore the smell of the hospital.

Our roles reversed, however, when Shawn was having contractions. I went into automatic protective mate mode. I let him clench my hand as hard as he could, swear at me until his cheeks were bright red, and threaten to burn down the whole hospital. I channeled Nicole's vibe and put on my most soothing voice, counted out his breaths, and told him he was doing a fantastic job. I was shocked that it always seemed to work, calming him down and helping him focus on his breathing. He walked around the room, took a warm shower, and squatted down to relieve the pressure. Finally, there was hardly any time between contractions, nurses were rushing in and out of the room, and someone declared he was fully dilated.

Maddie came back with her full team and brought lamps and medical equipment with her.

"Standing?" she asked, rubbing Shawn's back as he leaned over the delivery table and breathed through his latest contraction.

"Whatever it takes," he groaned.

"Well, then. Let's deliver this cub."

Half an hour of swearing, grunting, and sweating later, Shawn delivered a perfectly healthy, big, strong, wailing baby.

"Oh." It was about as much as I could say, stunned as I saw my son for the first time.

Shawn collapsed forward onto the bed, and I quickly grabbed him as Maddie cut the umbilical cord and then handed our baby boy to a nurse. I helped Shawn lie down, and wiped the tears from his face as I looked into his eyes. My heart swelled as he smiled at me with the most joyful expression on his face.

"I can't believe I just had a baby," he whispered.

"You did, sweetheart," I said, pride thrumming through my whole body.

"Here he is—healthy, fat, and beautiful," Maddie said, carrying our son over to the bed. He was quiet now as she placed him into Shawn's arms. My mate took a deep breath and let out a long, happy sigh of gratitude.

"He's perfect.".

"He *is* perfect," I said, looking down at his tiny face. "I thought he'd have your nose, but it looks like Cole's. And everything else is all you."

"Do you think so?" Shawn asked.

"Oh, yes. Like I said, perfect." Shawn smiled, and I leaned down to give him a little kiss.

"Do we have a name?" Maddie asked, beaming down at the little boy.

"Samuel," Shawn said softly, never taking his eyes off our son.

I smiled and nodded, reaching out and running a thumb over his cheek. "Samuel Kyle."

***

Once Shawn and Samuel were settled in, I walked out to the waiting room. Everyone looked up expectantly, and I could barely manage to hold back my excitement.

"Everything okay?" Bryce asked quickly. I bit down on my bottom lip and nodded happily, a little bit lost for words.

"Yes!" Jaxon cheered, and the whole group applauded. Even Lori let out a happy gurgle.

"He's so beautiful! He's just—wow!"

"Shawn or the baby?" Gavin asked with a chuckle.

"Both," I announced.

"It's a boy, right?" Cole asked.

"Yes, he's a boy. Want to come and meet your little brother?" I asked as I blinked tears out of my eyes.

Cole immediately bounded off the couch and ran over to me for a quick hug, and then power walked down the hall.

"Wrong way!" I called, laughing as he turned around without hesitation and marched in the order direction.

Back in the delivery room, Shawn lifted Samuel up and let me take him from his arms. I snuggled our baby for a moment then carried him over to Cole who was sitting patiently in a chair. As I placed our bundle down on Cole's lap, my heart felt like it was at absolute maximum capacity.

It was on the verge of exploding when Cole bent down and kissed his new brother on the cheek and whispered, "I'm going to take care of you no matter what. You'll always be my best friend."

"Oh shit," I swore, unable to take any more.

Shawn and Cole looked at me and I looked up at the ceiling, trying to hold back the tears. "I love you all so much," I said, sobbing all over again.

Both Shawn and Cole laughed and cried at the same time. "We love you too."

I couldn't believe how good things could be. My whole family, finally together. My fated mate, and our sons. There was just one member missing... LuLu.

Chapter 20 - Shawn

LuLu was at doggie daycare when I went into labor, and Trevor had sweetly agreed to keep her overnight for no extra charge. My coworkers had fixed it so I could stay at the hospital for a whole week if I'd wanted, but by the third day I was more than ready to get the hell out of there. Linc was visibly uncomfortable there too, constantly covering his nose with his hand whenever he came to visit. I kind of got what he meant, now my senses were heightened—it did smell pretty gross in there, but I still thought he was overreacting.

Samuel slept through the nights like a perfect angel, and he was a big eater already. He did a great job with the formula and had only lost a little bit of water weight by the time we were discharged from the hospital. Linc drove us to the homestead and got us set up in the nursery together before he went to get LuLu. Cole was staying with his mom, and I enjoyed how quiet the house was as I relaxed in the rocking chair with Samuel in my arms. It was so peaceful up here. It was barely out of town, but it felt like we were miles away from civilization. I let out a soft sigh of satisfaction as I gazed down at the little miracle in my arms.

He was so perfect, and I simply couldn't believe how much I loved him. I thought my love for Linc was next-level, but this was a whole different thing. Maybe it was my wolf growing more powerful inside me, but I felt so protective of Samuel. I would truly kill a man to protect him, with no hesitation.

He curled his hands into tiny fists and yawned, and I just about died from how cute it was. As he fell back to sleep, I closed my eyes and concentrated on my wolf. I was always aware of it, just there in the background, but now it came to the fore, taking me a little by surprise at how natural it felt. I'd expected it would take some practice to get fully used to it, but it was like my wolf had always been there, and now he was just as protective over Samuel as I was.

A little while later, I heard Linc's truck pull up to the house. I loved how easily I could hear the patter of LuLu's paws on the porch, and then the creak of the back door opening. I opened my eyes as the footsteps grew louder, and then Linc poked his head into the nursery. A huge smile spread over his face as he spotted the two of us.

"We're back," he said, rather unnecessarily.

LuLu popped her head around the doorway too. She offered a big doggy grin, and her tail started wagging like crazy when she spotted me.

"Hey, Lu!" I said, encouraging her to come in. She trotted over and sniffed gently at my legs. She could tell there was something interesting in my lap, and I couldn't wait to show her.

"She's not going to get jealous, is she?" Linc asked as he knelt down and scratched LuLu's back. She panted and sniffed harder at my knees.

"I don't think so," I said. "I mean, she's already been putting up with you taking all of my attention for over nine months."

Linc laughed and shook his head. LuLu put her paws up on my knees, and I watched her face as she spotted Samuel. She cocked her head to the side, and sniffed like crazy, but she quickly sat back on her butt and looked up at me like she was waiting for a command.

"Come up here, silly girl, it's okay, you can meet him." She quickly jumped back up and balanced with her paws on my knees. She sniffed the baby again and her tail started to furiously wag. "Well, I guess that means she likes him," I said.

"Who wouldn't? Everyone loves him," Linc replied proudly.

I let LuLu completely absorb Sam's scent so she'd quickly come to recognize him, and then when she dropped back down, I looked up at Linc. "Would you put him down for me?" I asked.

Linc scooped up Samuel from my arms as LuLu intently watched every move he made, never taking her eyes off Sam. Linc placed our baby gently into his crib and leaned down to kiss him. I hauled myself up out of the rocking chair and stood beside my mate, looking down at our little cub. LuLu put her front paws up on the side of the crib so she could keep an eye on Sam too.

I ran my hand over Linc's muscular back and felt a thrill of arousal move through me. I leaned against him and placed a soft kiss on the crook of his neck. He moaned softly and craned his neck so I could land more kisses there, and I happily obliged, trailing my lips up and down his neck. Linc let out a needy sigh and moved so that he could bring me closer and press a firm kiss against my mouth. I whimpered at how good it felt, and kissed him back, hard and deep. I moaned again when he began sucking softly on my bottom lip.

Suddenly, he pulled away. "Six weeks, right?" he asked with a strong sting of frustration in his voice.

"Ugh," I groaned. "Yeah, six weeks until I can have sex."

"That sounds like an eternity," he said, pushing his fingers through my hair.

"Well, as I tell my patients, it's better to wait than cause any issues. Anyway, there are other things we can do while we wait..."

"Oh yeah?" A spark lit Linc's toffee colored eyes, making them soft and warm.

I nodded, grinning up at him. "But first, there's something exciting I want to show you." I stepped back and he tilted his head to the side. LuLu did too, and I gave them both a reassuring smile before I closed my eyes and focused inward. I took a deep breath and felt for my wolf. I was sure I could do it. All I had to do was allow him out.

When I opened my eyes I could see the tight weave of cotton of Linc's pants in high definition, and the smell of his cologne smacked me so hard I reeled back. He gasped, and the sound of it made the fur inside my ears stand on end. I looked up to find him staring down at me with an expression of absolute glee.

I tried to speak, but all that came out was an excited yap. I suddenly felt a cold sensation on my rump and spun around to find LuLu sniffing my gray and black speckled flank. She jumped back, then lowered her head in submission. I felt my heart surge with compassion for her, and I nudged her with my snout to let her know I was still her friend. Then I felt the same kind of nudge against my side. I spun back the other way and was face to face with a wolf... With Linc. His amber eyes burned into mine, and every part of my fur-covered, long-limbed body felt drawn to him. I ran my snout against his, and he pushed back, nuzzling into me and licking at the fur on my neck. I whined low in my throat, and Linc's wolf moved back. Before I knew what he was going to do, he shifted back into his human form. Looking up at him I felt a surge of panic as I suddenly wondered if I'd remember how to be human. Maybe I'd be stuck as a wolf forever. But just as quickly as the panic came, it left, and I found myself standing on two legs, a little wobbly and light headed, but totally human.

"How did it feel?" Linc asked as he ran his hands over my shoulders.

"It was uh... Well... It just felt normal? Isn't that strange?"

Linc laughed. "That's your normal, now."

I took his hand and squeezed it. "I really like my normal now."

I was just about to lead Linc to our bedroom and show him what could be done in bed without breaking the doctor's orders, when Linc's phone rang. He stepped out of the nursery to answer the call, and I heard him talking to Jaxon. I wondered what he could be calling Linc for, and assumed it was to see if we got home safely from the hospital. When I heard Linc raise his voice, however, I realized the call was about something else.

I followed after Linc, closing the nursery door softly behind me. The baby monitor was turned on, and there were several receivers around the house, including our bedroom, but as I saw Linc, his jaw tight and his lips set into a thin line, I didn't think we'd be heading there just yet.

"What is it?" I asked when Linc hung up his phone.

"Jaxon just got a call from Steve Daniels, one of the pack who is a police detective. Some dragons have been spotted in the town causing trouble, and Jaxon wanted to know if I was willing to go out with them and see what's going on."

"Dragons? Did you just say, *dragons*?" I barely managed to keep my voice low so as not to disturb Sam, but LuLu whined as she identified the note of shock in my voice. What the fuck?

"Oh, yeah, right, I haven't told you about them have I? Well, sweetheart, wolves aren't the only shifters in town."